Copyright © L.C. Mawson (2016). All rights reserved. No part of this publication may be reproduced, distributed, or transmitted in any form or by any means, including photocopying, recording, or other electronic or mechanical methods, without the prior written permission of the publisher, except in the case of brief quotations embodied in critical reviews and certain other noncommercial uses permitted by copyright law.

This is a work of fiction. Names, characters, businesses, places, events and incidents are either the products of the author's imagination or used in a fictitious manner. Any resemblance to actual persons, living or dead, or actual events is purely coincidental.

The Lady Ruth Constance Chapelstone Chronicles

The Clockwork Suitor
The Parisian Thief
The American Escapade

The Freya Snow Series

Trapped
Hunt
Short Story Collection
White
Wings
Oracle
Witch
Enhanced

The Phoenix Saga

Heart of a Moon
Protector

L.C. Mawson

The condition we now refer to as 'autism' was first recognised by the medical communities of Europe in the first half of the 20th century.

However, before this point, Autistic people still existed. Many were simply seen as 'eccentric' and certain euphemisms arose to describe them.

One such euphemism arose during the Industrial Revolution, within the upper class of London. Many of the great minds behind the revolution were referred to as having 'an inventor's disposition'.

The majority of the modern day technology we so heavily rely on - particularly automatons and other mechanicals - can be traced back to these inventors.

One such inventor was referred to only as The Owl, and they were single-handedly responsible for a great deal of both technological and social change during Queen Victoria's reign.

- Excerpt from *The Owl: The Birth of the Automaton Age*, By Professor Lucinda Caroline Mawson

The Complete Lady Ruth Constance Chapelstone Chronicles

BOOK ONE
LADY RUTH AND THE CLOCKWORK SUITOR

L.C. Mawson

1

Somewhere just south of York, Lady Ruth Constance Chapelstone came to the conclusion that travelling by train did not agree with her.

Of course, she had never left her home city of Newcastle before, so she had no idea if the train was the offensive factor, or if it was simply travel itself. As her eyes ached and her stomach churned, however, she decided that the question of what exactly was offending her was immaterial. She was offended, and that was enough to turn her mood sour.

Her hair clips felt as if they were trying to dig into her skull, and her nose couldn't help but pick up even the slightest smell. Her only source of comfort was the familiar pressure of her corset tight around her middle, grounding her. But the comforting effect was slightly muted by the fact that the bright yellow colour of her dress was now too much for her eyes.

"How much longer until we reach London, Uncle Thomas?" she asked as soon as he stepped into the private carriage. Despite being her uncle, he was only a few years older than her. However, because he shared her dark hair and eyes — contrasted by fair skin — they were often mistaken for siblings and could easily pass as twins, probably because Ruth almost entirely took after her father. The only thing she inherited from her mother was thick, almost unmanageable, hair and a full figure.

"We are still in the north, my dear," he pointed out as he took the tray he was carrying and placed it down on the table between them.

Oh good, thought Ruth, *he brought tea.*

Someone else should have probably brought them the tea, in all honesty, but Ruth was in no fit state to deal with strangers, and her uncle was more than accommodating. *An inventor's disposition,* he called it, simply taking it as the flip side to his greatest discovery.

When they had been younger, Thomas had taken to inventing for a while, as he had seen what the industrial revolution was doing for Britain and he wanted to play a hand in shaping the future.

He had been lousy at it, of course. Ruth had told him as much when she had visited his workshop. After a few hours of ravenously pouring through his textbooks while he brought her tea and biscuits, she had managed to fix up the invention that he had spent weeks stumped over, completely unable to get it to work as intended. After that, Thomas had given up inventing, fancying himself an entrepreneur instead, much to the chagrin of his father. Ruth had taken over his workshop, bearing some of the family disappointment so that it was no longer Thomas' sole domain. After all, the workshop was no proper place for a lady.

It didn't take Thomas long to realise that he could make them both rich by selling Ruth's inventions. Not that they needed the money, of course; that was simply Thomas' way of keeping score.

At her mother's insistence, no one knew that Ruth was behind Thomas' inventions. Thomas said that it was a shy friend of his — nicknamed The Owl for his penchant for only working at night — giving Thomas the perfect excuse not to introduce the inventor to his friends.

Much to everyone but Ruth and Thomas' surprise, it wasn't long before The Owl had the attention of Queen Victoria herself. As far as Ruth was concerned, it was inevitable. Her engine designs were far superior to anything the Crown had in operation, and her dirigible schematics were not only technically impressive, but far more eye-pleasing than anything currently in use.

If there was one thing The Owl had become notorious for, it was style. Ruth's penchant for fashion and design was as impressive as her knack for invention. It was simply a shame that nothing else held even the slightest interest for her. Her mother always said that, had they not had servants, Ruth would have no chance at survival.

Ruth briefly wondered if air travel would have been easier on her stomach, or, if not, if there was some way for her to alter her designs to make it so that it was.

Her attention was drawn back to the present as Thomas flipped the switch at the side of the bulky mechanism cradling the teapot. It made a whirring noise as it lifted up the pot and began to pour the tea, causing the pot to clink against the cup in a way that made Ruth whine in protest. Her ears were exceptionally delicate. As was the rest of her, for that matter.

"This tea of yours had better not offend my palette," Thomas told her as he passed her a cup.

She ignored the sugar in favour of milk. She couldn't stand sugar in her tea, and only even used the milk to cool it so that she didn't burn herself. She had a tendency to forget how hot tea was in her eagerness to drink it.

"It's not my fault if your palette is easily offended."

He raised an eyebrow at that, and Ruth had to concede that it had been hypocritical of her. While she had broad taste in tea, she was very particular with her food. In fact, the cook at home had resigned herself to making the same three dishes for Ruth, with no variance. She supposed that was a luxury she may not be granted in London. Even if she had the same dish there, it probably wouldn't be right.

She drank the tea immediately after adding her milk. It was still hot enough to provide her with the scorching sensation she craved, while not burning her insides. The ginger in the chai helped to settle her stomach.

Thomas pulled a face.

"Not to your liking?" she asked as she poured herself a second cup.

"No," he told her firmly. "But it is no matter. I am far less interested in the topic of tea than the topic of what great invention The Owl has to show my contacts in London. They have already seen your previous work, so we'll need something fresh and exciting."

"I have actually been working on something. For Grandfather."

"For my father?" Thomas asked with a raised eyebrow as Ruth brought out a series of schematics.

"I have a prototype in one of my cases," she assured him as she found the correct piece of paper, "but this is the design."

"It's… a leg."

"Yes. A fully functioning, clockwork leg."

"And how exactly would the leg know when to move and when to remain still?"

Ruth sighed into her, again empty, teacup. "That is what I am still working on. I have several ideas. Perhaps a control of some sort. I could possibly program it to move as the stump moves in a specific way. I have also been reading about the possibility of measuring the information sent by the brain to the limbs. I could perhaps make use of that…"

"Careful not to get too carried away with theoretical ideas," Thomas reminded her, as he so often did. Ruth never listened, but he kept reminding her anyway.

"When will we be in London?" she asked again, eager to be off the train.

"I'll find you some more tea," was Thomas' only reply.

2

The first word Ruth would use to describe London was *crowded*.

That wasn't a good sign.

The second would be *putrid*, which wasn't any better. Of course, all cities had a certain stench about them, but she was used to Newcastle. She wasn't sure if London smelled objectively worse, but she knew that it was different, which was enough to upset her.

Between the oppressive atmosphere and her lingering nausea from the train, Ruth was close to tears.

She hovered on the step of the train, waiting until the crowds on the platform dissipated a bit before getting off.

"It's King's Cross," Thomas told her gently as he realised what she was doing. "It's never quieter than this."

Ruth made a small noise of annoyance in the back of her throat before steeling herself and stepping down onto the platform. She distracted herself from the bustle around her by focusing on the large mechanical arms unloading the luggage from the train.

Watching the gears turn was calming, even if she couldn't help but criticise the design as she looked it over.

Clunky. Inelegant. Clumsy.

She wondered if there was a single engineer besides herself with even the slightest inclination towards style.

Luckily, Thomas predicted her discomfort, and had a carriage waiting for them. At the front was a mechanical driver, if such an unwieldy contraption could even be considered a *driver*. It clearly directed the horses, but they had made no effort to make it look even vaguely humanoid.

It looked like a box with metal, spider-like arms out of the side, and a speaker on the front.

"LORD CHAPELSTONE," it greeted with a grating voice that made Ruth tighten her fists around the fabric of her skirt.

"Yes," Thomas replied. "You are our ride?"

"INPUT NOT RECOGNISED. PLEASE RESTATE REQUEST."

Ruth couldn't help but roll her eyes. "It's a Fralsen, Thomas. Fifth model, by the look of it. You would have an easier time trying to converse with a stray cat."

"Then what shall we do?"

"Get in and hope it takes us somewhere where I can lie down," Ruth told him firmly. She was quite fed up and just wanted to curl into bed.

Thomas nodded, acquiescing, before helping her into the carriage.

The driver thankfully managed to take them to Thomas' house in the city without any issue. Ruth's travel sickness had returned by the time they left the carriage, despite the short journey.

Ruth noted that said house was modest compared to home, but she didn't care. She just wanted to be inside.

"Workshop?" she asked as soon as she was through the door. Her tiredness immediately fled as she remembered Thomas promising her a workshop worthy of her talents.

Her uncle smiled. "In just a moment. I want to introduce you to someone."

As soon as the door closed behind them, a young woman hurried down the stairs. She was wearing a plain brown dress that was just a few shades lighter than her dark skin. Her black hair was tied back, forming a fluffy cloud to the back of her head. She didn't look older than sixteen.

"Ruth, this is Ivy. When I first visited London, she approached me and begged to work with The Owl."

"So, she knows?"

"No, I thought I would leave that up to you. But I won't be here all of the time, so I suggest a trade. The Owl takes her on as an apprentice and has someone to talk to about his inventions, and she makes sure that he doesn't starve himself."

Ruth smiled, though it was a little strained. She wasn't too sure that she wanted someone around her at all times, yet she had to admit that it would be nice to have some help from someone whose eyes wouldn't glaze over when she got too deep into the minutia of her designs.

"I suppose it is not too disagreeable an arrangement," Ruth said, turning to Ivy. "Could you show me to the workshop?"

Ivy nodded, showing her up the stairs until they reached the attic.

"This is the workshop, Milady," Ivy said in an almost painful cockney accent. That would take some getting used to.

Before she could dwell too much on it, however, Ruth spotted the selection of work benches and top-of-the-line tools. She had been good at making do when she lacked something, but the idea of not having to made her grin. How much time it would save!

"Oh, it's beautiful!" Ruth cried as she hurried back to where Thomas had just brought in their luggage, finding the case with her designs. She took as many as would fit in her arms before running back upstairs to affix them to the large board on the wall of her workshop.

"When will The Owl arrive?" Ivy asked, though Ruth didn't hear her, as she was too absorbed in deciding which project to start first.

"He just did," Thomas told her with a smile. "I suggest getting some tea for you and Lady Ruth. She is always more talkative when there is tea."

3

Ruth hated leaving her workshop, but some things could not be avoided. Introducing herself to London society was one of them. Ivy, much to Ruth's envy, had no such social expectations placed on her, allowing her to remain in the workshop to focus on her own projects.

Ivy had been shocked that Ruth allowed her to work on whatever she wanted, but in truth, it was simply convenient. Ruth didn't need help at all times, and she didn't want the pressure of feeling as if she had to entertain Ivy every second she was working. So, Ivy had her own projects to work on when Ruth didn't need her or was busy choosing a new dress.

"Smile, dear," Thomas reminded her as they arrived at Lady Dunsten's ball.

Ruth nodded, realising that she had been frowning in thought. She just really wanted to be back in her workshop. But there was a bright side; attending a ball had given her an excuse to buy a new dress, and the dark blue one she had on had one of the sturdiest corsets she had ever found.

"Thomas," greeted a man who looked just a little older than Ruth, with brownish red hair that extended into mutton chops and a very clean military uniform. "It's good to see you again."

"You too, James." Thomas gestured to Ruth. "This is my niece, Lady Chapelstone."

"Pleased to meet you," James greeted her with a smile, taking Ruth's hand to kiss. "Your uncle has mentioned you briefly, but he failed to mention your beauty."

Ruth felt a spike of irritation at that. She didn't want to deal with men fawning over her. That would mean rejecting them, which could get messy.

Ruth had never cared for *messy*.

She smiled, despite the irritation. "Why, thank you."

James, to Ruth's relief, turned back to Thomas. "So, you didn't bring The Owl with you?"

"No," James said. "He dislikes having to leave his workshop. You know how inventors are."

"I do, but Thomas… While his inventions are, without a doubt, the best, this is becoming a matter of security. If The Owl wishes to sell inventions to the Crown, I must at least meet him."

Thomas nodded, though Ruth wanted to scream at him to come with an excuse or a lie. Something — anything — to delay that possibility.

"I'm sure that can be arranged," Thomas said, deeply confusing Ruth.

"That would be much appreciated," James told him.

Before Ruth could protest, a woman approached, with the same reddish-brown hair and grey eyes as James.

"Are you two boring poor Lady Chapelstone with your talk of business?" she asked in a no-nonsense manner.

James stiffened, his brow furrowing ever so slightly. "This is my sister, Anne."

Anne moved over to Ruth, leading her away from the men. "Come on, dear, let's leave those two to talk. I'll introduce you to everyone."

Any protest from Ruth died on her tongue, her words draining away with her terror at the prospect of meeting new people without her uncle.

Anne had not been joking when she had said *everyone,* Ruth learnt as she was escorted throughout the room in a whirlwind of new names and faces, none of which she remembered. It took her almost an hour to slip her new guide, pretending to need to relieve herself. Instead she found a quiet corner and allowed herself a brief respite. It took several moments of focusing on her breathing and the comforting way her corset hugged her for the room to stop spinning.

"Had to slip away?"

Ruth jumped at the intrusion, though it was barely noticeable, thanks to her lethargy. She had to put what little energy she had recovered into her smile as James approached, passing her a glass of wine.

"I don't drink," she told him, eventually remembering to add, "But thank you for the thought."

He nodded in understanding. "Thomas mentioned that you weren't much for crowds."

Ruth didn't have anything to say to that, so she simply nodded.

"I'm sorry, I thought having my sister introduce you around would make things easier for you."

"It did," Ruth managed. It wasn't even a lie. Having Anne escort her had certainly been better than her standing mutely in a corner or constantly tailing Thomas as he talked with men, who would either look her over with unrestrained interest or ignore and condescend her.

"Anne is very nice." Ruth had no idea if that particular point was true or not; she had been so carefully keeping her attention on getting her social niceties correct with all of the other girls Anne had introduced her to that she hadn't had enough concentration to pay much attention to her guide. Definitely not enough to form an opinion on her. But she hadn't been sure of what else to say, so she had fabricated the positive opinion in the hopes of keeping James happy so that he wouldn't notice if she slipped.

James smiled. "I'm glad you enjoyed her company, Lady Chapelstone." He moved his mouth upwards at just one side in a way that Ruth couldn't quite decipher. "Your name is a tad long, may I call you Ruth?"

"My name is but four syllables," she pointed out, before realising that it was perhaps rude of her. She was unsure of how to decline without risking his ire, so she relented. "But, yes, you may call me Ruth."

His smile widened to become even on both sides. "Thank you, Ruth."

She nodded, curtly, wishing that she had something non-alcoholic to drink so that she could buy herself a little time before she was expected to speak once more.

Thankfully, Thomas chose that moment to find her.

"Are you having a nice time?" he asked.

"I am a little tired," she said, as she always did to indicate that she wished to be extracted.

Thomas nodded in understanding before turning to James. "We should take our leave. It's getting late, and Ruth requires her sleep."

"Of course. It was nice to see you both. Thomas, I shall send correspondence about meeting with The Owl."

"Of course," Thomas replied as they took their leave.

As soon as they were outside, Ruth turned to her uncle. "He can't meet The Owl."

"No, he can't, but it would be impolite to not at least seem to make the effort to arrange a meeting. I shall fob him off with excuses, and he shall eventually grow bored. If he wants the inventions, which he clearly does, he will forgo the meeting after a few failed attempts."

Ruth gave a disgruntled hum. It seemed like courting trouble to her, but her uncle was much better with people than she was.

4

"I think I've done it!" Ruth called out, bouncing up and down a little with excitement. Having Thomas around to appreciate her work had always been nice, but he had always seen it as an opportunity. As Ivy quickly bounded over, Ruth found herself glad to have someone who appreciated her work in the same way that she did.

"Done what? Can I see?"

Ruth nodded, taking Ivy by the shoulders and moving her back from the contraption she had just finished tinkering with. As usual, when Ruth got close, Ivy seemed to get a tad fidgety, causing Ruth to assume that she was shy.

Ruth took the box from the counter, which was connected to the mechanism by a long, thick cable.

Ruth moved the toggle on the box, and in response, the metal spindles that were connected to the bottom of an oval, looking almost like an oddly shaped table, moved with a clicking sound, going from side to side.

"It's like a spider!" Ivy exclaimed with fascination, taking a timid step towards the contraption.

Ruth nodded. "They're legs. Should someone lose their own, they could control these new ones with this box."

"Should they not look more… human?"

Ruth blinked. "Why? This is far more efficient."

Ivy shrugged. "I suppose, but I imagine many people would be attached to how their human legs look."

Ruth hummed in thought before nodding. "Perhaps you're right. This is what I enjoy about having you here, Ivy. You're good at giving me a fresh perspective on my work."

Ivy grinned as Ruth went back over to the spider legs to adjust one that was slightly out of sync with the others.

"What about your other project?" Ivy asked, moving over to the workbench.

"Oh, the mechanical brain? It's progressing. I have it capable of simple arithmetic, but it's a chore. I'm trying to build the system from the ground up, rather than basing it on the Fralsen system, which I believe to be inherently flawed."

"Could you use some help with it?" Ivy asked, inching closer to the invention, though she didn't dare touch it.

"I suppose some input wouldn't go amiss."

Before Ivy could respond, a loud knock echoed from below. Ruth froze at the unexpected noise, her fists clenching as she realised that it meant unexpected visitors.

"I'll answer it," Ivy said before rushing downstairs to greet their guest.

Ruth couldn't cope with any more household staff than Ivy, but it would have been unseemly for either her or Thomas to answer. Ivy, thankfully, didn't seem to mind helping them keep up appearances, though Ruth suspected that had to do with how well Thomas was paying her.

"Lord Holly," Ivy said, loud enough for it to carry upstairs.

Ruth frowned, not recognising the name.

Thomas, who had been in his downstairs study, hurried out, and Ruth saw from her spot at the top of the stairs that he was inviting James inside, recognising him by his muttonchops.

"I'm dreadfully sorry for stopping by unannounced," James said, though Ruth didn't think that he sounded sorry at all. "I was nearby and thought that this may be an opportune time for me to meet The Owl."

Ivy raced back upstairs as Thomas began to make excuses.

"Your clothes, Ma'am," she hissed.

Ruth looked down to see that her plain dress, apron and gloves were covered in grease. James would know immediately that she had been the one in the workshop if he saw her.

"Quickly," Ruth said, hurrying to her room and waving for Ivy to follow her. "Help me get changed. I will not be able to lace up quickly enough on my own."

Ivy did as she was told, though she moved stiffly as she did so. Ruth wondered if the poor girl was ill, though she pushed the thought away. She didn't need to be worrying about contracting anything from her assistant when she had so much else to be concerned with.

Ruth quickly stripped off her skirts as soon as the door shut behind her.

"Could you bring me a clean dress?" she asked Ivy, who hurried across the room to her wardrobe.

Ivy hesitated as she brought the blue dress back to Ruth, who had stripped down to her underskirts.

"What is it?" Ruth asked, impatiently placing her hands on her hips.

"I... Nothing," Ivy squeaked, not quite looking at Ruth.

Ruth didn't quite believe her, but took her word as Ivy helped her to scramble into the dress and lace up, though Ivy was noticeably hesitant as her fingers neared Ruth's skin, putting Ruth a little on edge.

She wished Ivy wasn't so damn shy.

As soon as Ruth was laced up properly, she raced out of her room, just as James was making his way up the stairs.

"The Owl doesn't like to be disturbed while he's working!" Thomas protested, following quickly behind James.

"Just a quick introduction, Thomas. Then this can all move along."

Ruth stepped forward, drawing James' attention.

"I'm afraid The Owl stepped out for a bit," she said before James reached the door of the workshop.

"Stepped out?"

"He went for a walk to clear his head. He does that from time to time when he's looking for inspiration."

"How long do you think he will be gone?"

She shrugged. "Maybe an hour, maybe the rest of the night. You know how inventors are. It would most likely be a waste of your time to wait for him."

James nodded. "I'm sorry for my intrusion, Ruth. I simply thought that it would be best to get my meeting The Owl out of the way. I suspect he may try to put me off forever, and I am a busy man."

"He is quite shy. Perhaps you should forgo the meeting, given that Thomas can vouch for him."

"I wish that I could, but there are strict protocols on the matter. If I cannot meet The Owl, the Crown cannot use his inventions."

"That would be a pity."

"Indeed," James said before turning back to Thomas. "If you could let me know when you expect him to be home, I shall try to stop by. I know you want to protect your friend, but this is a necessity and putting it off will not help."

Thomas nodded. "I shall redouble my efforts to arrange a meeting."

"I would be most grateful," James said, before turning back to Ruth. "And I would be most delighted to see you again."

"Oh, if you drop by to see The Owl, I'm sure you will," she said, her tone betraying nothing, though she meant her words as a subtle barb to her uncle. Not that he would pick up on it, but it made her feel better.

As soon as the front door closed behind James, Ruth glared at Thomas, her arms folded tightly across her chest.

"Your approach isn't working."

To her irritation, her uncle simply replied with a mild, "Apparently not."

5

Ruth felt discomforted by her lack of corset. She had always liked the constant pressure around her middle, and she greatly missed it. But wearing one would ruin the illusion she was going for.

The fabric around her chest, binding it down, wasn't the same. In fact, it felt uncomfortable around her rather generous bosom.

"How do I look?" Ruth asked Ivy, as she twirled around in Thomas' clothes.

"I think you look rather dashing."

Ruth smiled as she placed a hat over her pinned up hair, pulling it down over her eyes so that she wouldn't be recognised.

She paused as she heard the front door open. Ivy hurried out of the room to double check that it was Thomas, before coming back and giving a nod of affirmation.

Ruth grinned, rushing out of the room and downstairs as her uncle was still taking off his coat.

"Ruth?" Thomas asked as he saw her.

Her heart sank in disappointment at being recognised, before realising that no one else would likely be in the house. And Thomas had known her all her life; just because he recognised her didn't mean that others would.

"No," she said, forcing her voice low. "I'm The Owl."

Thomas rolled his eyes. "Ruth, you're never going to fool anyone with that disguise."

"I might," she said, forgetting about making her voice low.

"Ruth, your face is too soft, and you're quite recognisable. Especially to someone like James who knows how to pay attention."

"Ivy thought it was a good disguise," she countered, folding her arms.

Ivy cleared her throat before speaking up. "Well, no. I said you looked dashing, not that you would fool anyone."

Ruth sighed. "Well, we have to do something."

"No, we don't," Thomas said, shaking his head a little. "James will let it slide eventually. We just have to have patience."

"If he's so willing to let it slide, why was he here in the middle of the night?"

Thomas did a poor job of holding back a smirk. "Well, to start, it wasn't that late. The Londoners tend to stay up a little later than we do back home. And is it not obvious why he was here?"

"To see The Owl."

"No, to see you, Ruth. If he wasn't so smitten with you, he most likely wouldn't have stopped by."

"Smitten?"

"You hadn't noticed? James has every intention of courting you."

"Oh," Ruth said with a frown, the unexpected information causing her brain to freeze. "But I don't want that."

"Then reject him. Perhaps you should wait until after the contract has been signed, though. Just in case."

Ruth's frown deepened, despite Thomas' reassurance that rejecting James was an option. "Would he really do such a thing? Be so petty?"

"I was joking," Thomas clarified. "Mostly."

Ruth huffed as she finally removed her hat; it was getting in the way of her vision.

"Though you may want to reconsider his offer. James is good man, and he will be only the first of many. You will have to start considering the prospect of marriage soon."

"Why?"

"Why? Well, because you'll have to marry eventually and you're hardly getting any younger."

"Neither are you," Ruth countered with a pout. "And you're the one who has to carry on the family name."

"Let me worry about that."

"Then let me worry about my own future. I don't want to get married. I have no interest in it."

"You're only saying that because no one has caught your interest."

"Perhaps, but at this point, I doubt anyone ever will. And I'm not upset by that. The only thing about it I don't like is that everyone else thinks I should be perturbed by my lack of romantic attraction."

Thomas nodded in understanding. "I'm sorry. I shouldn't have pushed. If you don't want to marry, no one should force you to."

"Thank you."

Thomas smiled. "Perhaps you should change out of that outfit and into something more appropriate. Believe me, we shall find a solution to this that is a little less theatrical."

Ruth nodded before heading back upstairs with Ivy trailing behind her.

"Ruth?" Ivy asked as Ruth focused on the buttons of her waistcoat.

"Hmm?"

"Did you mean what you said to Thomas? About never wanting to get married?"

"Of course. I wouldn't have said it if I didn't mean it. Why?"

"Nothing, I just… Do you really never feel attracted to anyone? Never get giddy at the thought of simply holding their hand?"

"No," Ruth said, a little shortly. "And I don't see how that's a problem. I'm not needed to continue the family name, and romance just seems more trouble than it's worth beyond that. I have Thomas and I have you. Friends and family. What more could I need?"

"You truly think of me as a friend?"

"Well, I suppose so, yes. Why?"

"I just- I… It's nothing. I'm grateful."

Ruth frowned. "Grateful? Why?"

"Well, it's just, you're… You're *you*. You're The Owl and I'm just some kid…"

Ruth's frown deepened. "I don't understand. Are you saying a friendship between us is unlikely because of our age difference?"

"No. Well, yes, a little. And our difference in social status." Ruth, oblivious as always, missed the way that Ivy waved to her face when she spoke, indicating that she was talking about more than just her class.

"Huh. I suppose I never really gave that any thought."

"And you're so…"

"So…?"

Ivy shook her head, seemingly unable to finish that sentence.

"I enjoy having someone to talk about my inventions with," Ruth reasoned, as a way of explaining. "And other things as well, I suppose."

"Then I am happy to be your friend," Ivy said, finally settling Ruth's unease at the strange conversation.

6

Explosions weren't Ruth's preferred method of breaking her focus so that she would remember to eat, but she had to admit, as she and Ivy struggled to cough away the plume of smoke that had engulfed them, it worked about as well as anything else.

"What the devil happened up here?" Thomas asked as he bounded up the stairs to where the women were coughing in the hallway.

"We were experimenting," Ivy told him. "Trying to get the steam less conspicuous. The mechanical brain creates far too much."

"Mechanical brain?" Thomas asked with a raised eyebrow.

"Well, if you don't mind the soot, I could show you," Ruth said, giving up on her dress. It was definitely ruined but it, thankfully, wasn't one of her good ones. She had quickly learnt her lesson regarding proper attire in the workshop.

Thomas narrowed his eyes in a way that suggested that he very much would mind the soot.

"It's very impressive," Ivy told him.

"Alright, fine. But I think you two are in need of a break. After you've shown me, you two should get cleaned up and I'll take you out for lunch."

Ruth hated eating out of the house, but Ivy was instantly ecstatic and she couldn't bring herself to ruin the younger woman's excitement.

"So, what exactly does this mechanical brain do?" Thomas asked as they entered the workshop.

Ruth began quickly wiping the soot off of it and making sure that none of it had gotten into the delicate systems housed within. Thankfully, everything seemed to be in order, she found as she tested it manually before closing the casing back up.

She went to the speaker and microphone next to each other on the table, both wired up to the brain.

"Can you understand me?" Ruth asked into the microphone.

"YES," came the voice from the speaker. She had, unfortunately, had to use the Fralsen voice box temporarily, but she felt that she could tweak it in order to make it less grating.

"So it's something to rival the Fralsens?" Thomas asked with a hum. "It will have to be good to disrupt their monopoly. People have been trying for years and no one is close."

"If anyone can get there, it's me," Ruth told him as she placed her hands on her hips before returning to the microphone. "Can you identify me?"

"ANALYSIS OF VOCAL PATTERNS SUGGEST THAT YOU ARE LADY RUTH CONSTANCE CHAPELSTONE. ALIAS: THE OWL."

"Should it have that information?" Thomas asked. "Who knows who it will tell."

"Don't worry, no one outside of this room will see it until I'm sure that it is up to my standards, which means that it will be more than capable of keeping the information to itself." She turned to face Thomas with a glare, her hands still on her hips. "You're not being excited. This is exciting."

"This is potentially promising," he corrected her. "Exciting is a bit of a stretch."

"It recognised me based on vocal patterns. How is that not exciting?"

"Given that you and Ivy are the only two I can safely assume it has interacted with, and Ivy, no offence intended, has a particularly strong cockney accent, it's not that exciting."

Ruth sighed. "I thought it was exciting," she grumbled as she returned to trying to salvage her dress.

"And I'm sure that I will also find it exciting once it actually rivals a Fralsen," Thomas assured her. "And once you have solved the steam issue."

"Ah, yes, well, about that. I was actually thinking about using aether instead."

"No," Thomas said immediately.

"Thomas, I can't get what I need from steam alone."

"Yes, but I would very much like the house to remain in one piece."

"I can be careful."

"This explosion says otherwise."

"Thomas, please. Fralsen will surely be using aether within the next few years. We have to start now if we want to be competitive."

Thomas sighed, pinching the bridge of his nose. "Fine," he eventually said. "I shall see about getting you an aether core, but I can't promise anything." He turned to Ivy. "If you get changed, we'll go out for lunch now."

Ivy nodded, hurrying out of the room.

"She seems more comfortable around you," Thomas noted.

Ruth nodded. "I know I am not the most personable. I'm just glad that she appears to be used to me now."

"Oh, I don't think that was ever her problem."

"There's no need to make me feel better, Thomas. I know that I am an acquired taste."

"I'm not saying it to make you feel better, Ruth."

She frowned. "Then what do you mean?"

He sighed, folding his arms. "I mean that Ivy is a young woman who admired The Owl immensely, to the point at which she actively sought me out in order to work with him. She's bright, in an environment that doesn't value such things. I would put good money on her daydreaming of one day approaching The Owl and convincing him to take her on as his assistant. After many a late night toiling in the workshop together, he would be the first person to truly appreciate her worth."

"And? Isn't that what happened?" Ruth's frown deepened. She was very confused.

"Well, yes, that's my point."

"What's your point?"

Thomas sighed. "My point was that she probably had an amorous affection for The Owl."

"Oh! So, she was disappointed when I turned out to be a woman?"

"Ivy doesn't strike me as the type to discriminate when it comes to gender. I think she was more disappointed when you revealed that you were never attracted to anyone."

"Oh," Ruth said, feeling a little bad. She liked Ivy and didn't want to have hurt her, no matter how unintentionally. "Well, perhaps Ivy should come with me next time I'm invited to some tedious social event. It would be far more interesting to help her to find a suitor than to force myself to make small talk."

Thomas gave her a curious look.

"What?"

"Well… Are you not disturbed by the fact that she's attracted to women as well as men?"

"No. She's my friend."

Thomas just kept on staring at her, before eventually saying, "Is it truly that simple for you?"

"She's my friend," Ruth repeated.

In truth, she hadn't had many friends before, but she saw little that would make her turn on those she had.

"I had better hurry and get changed, otherwise Ivy will be furious at having to wait for lunch," she said, deciding that she was done with the draining conversation.

7

"What's this?" Ivy asked as Ruth passed her a bundle of dark blue fabric after they were done with their afternoon tea.

"A dress," Ruth told her. "I thought that you should come with me to the ball tonight."

Ivy shifted a little from one foot to the other, biting her lip as she looked over the dress.

"I really appreciate this, Ruth, but... I can't accept it. The other people at the ball will take one look at me and know that I don't belong. And I'm okay with that. I don't want to spend an evening having them sneer at me."

Ruth sighed, nodding as she folded her arms. "In truth, I don't want that either. I'm not... I'm not good at making friends. As much as Thomas will be there, he often gets sucked into the crowd. Not to mention the number of men who will seek my attention."

"Just start kicking 'em in the groin if they give you too much hassle. Always worked for me."

"I fear that would be more likely to make me a social pariah than anything else."

"At least pariahs don't have to go to balls they don't want to."

"Well, no. But I'm pretty sure my mother's response would be to come down here herself to set me straight, and that is the last thing I want."

"Not get on with your folks?"

"We have little in common. Except, perhaps, a passion for being well dressed, though our opinions on what that phrase means often differ drastically."

"Harsh. I've always gotten on well with my mum."

"And she approves of you working with me?"

"She can't complain with what Thomas has been paying me."

"No, I suppose not." Ruth sighed once more. "Are you sure you won't accompany me?"

"I don't think that I've ever been more sure of anything else."

A single hour into the ball, Ruth was ready to leave. The cacophony of music and chatter was giving her a headache and she was struggling to remain expressive.

"You're making quite a few friends tonight," Thomas noted as she sidled back up to him, hoping to convince him to take her back home.

"I am quite the thespian when I put my mind to it," she replied with a tight smile. "But it's getting late and I'm getting tired."

"Ah. Of course."

Ruth let Thomas make the farewells as she started to feel lightheaded. She desperately needed fresh air. It was a pity that there was so little of it in the city.

She clutched at her skirts, her fist grabbing and letting go of the fabric to a rhythm that soothed her, if only a little.

Thomas hailed a Fralsen-driven carriage to escort them home.

"WHERE WOULD YOU LIKE TO BE TAKEN?" the Fralsen shouted in its usual, grating voice.

Ruth let out a squeal of protest, her hands flapping against her skirts as she spun away from the noise.

"Ruth? Ruth, it's okay," Thomas tried to assure her, moving his hand to her arm.

She slapped it away, her words not coming fast enough for a gentler rebuke as her attempt to settle her hands seemed to have the effect of transferring her frustrated energy into tears.

She was crying in the middle of the street in a completely undignified fashion, but she wasn't quite ready to share the confined space of the carriage with Thomas just yet.

"I'm tired," she managed, in a feeble attempt at apology.

"I'm sorry. I shouldn't have kept you out so late."

She shrugged. "I didn't say anything. I thought I could manage until we got home."

She wiped away her tears with her handkerchief before hurrying to the carriage. The sooner they got home, the sooner she could hide.

As soon as Ruth was home, she silently made her way to the workshop. Thomas, thankfully, knew enough to leave her alone.

She turned on the mechanical brain as soon as she entered the workshop, as had become her habit when Ivy wasn't there. It needed to practice talking if it was ever going to rival a Fralsen.

"Good evening, Mech," she said. Ivy had suggested the nickname, since "the mechanical brain" was a bit of a mouthful.

"Good evening, Lady Ruth," it replied in a tone far more melodic and soothing than the grating yells of the Fralsens. "Have you had a pleasant day?"

She knew that it was a preprogrammed question, but it still lightened her heart a little.

"Not really," she confessed. "I stayed too long at the ball and… Well, I had somewhat of an episode when I finally left."

"An episode?"

She shrugged, forgetting that it couldn't see. "When I get frustrated, it's as if I'm a bottle of champagne that has been shaken too much. If not allowed proper time to rest, I simply explode. It does not help that I am so delicate as to be easily frustrated by unexpected noises or unpleasant textures. It leads to many a night like tonight."

"That is not normal human behaviour?"

"No. No, it is not."

Mech didn't seem to have a response to that and Ruth didn't blame it. She had only programmed it for so many responses and she was sure that most people would struggle to come up with something to say to her in that moment.

"It's fine, Mech," she assured it. "I simply need to be better about my limits." Ruth hummed. "Actually, you might be able to help me track trends. If I can figure out when I am most vulnerable, I can plan my social calendar more effectively."

"I would be happy to help."

Ruth smiled, despite knowing that there was no way Mech could deny her request. It wasn't a person; it was just a machine, but it was comforting to think otherwise.

She wished that Mech could accompany her out of the workshop. As much as she didn't leave that often, it would have been comforting to talk to someone who wasn't a real someone when she was frustrated. It would take away the embarrassment, which always delayed her calming down.

She moved over to the collection of projects she had been working on, humming as she went. It mostly consisted of a selection of clockwork limbs she had built to help amputees, like her grandfather. There were also a few plans for internal organs, but they were in the most initial stages. She needed a firmer grasp of biology before pursuing them.

But movement? Movement she had perfected.

How hard would it be to construct a human looking vessel for Mech?

She hummed as she started to get to work, and Mech joined in with chimes that sounded almost like a music box.

8

"What's all that?" Ruth asked, as she and Ivy drank their tea with Thomas. He had started insisting on them all having afternoon tea together in an effort to see more of Ruth. With Mech's progress coming along so well, she barely left the workshop. Its body was nearly complete and quite human looking, and its mind was capable of mimicking an almost natural conversation.

Thomas put down one of the many letters he was rifling through. "I have been contacted by many of my friends in recent months."

"Really?"

"Yes. In fact, almost every unmarried friend who has met you has contacted me, enquiring about your availability."

"Availability? We're talking about marriage again? I thought I had been firm on the matter."

Thomas sighed as Ivy stared at her teacup in an attempt to stay out of the conversation that was so blatant that even Ruth picked up on it.

"I am simply telling you that they have shown interest. I'm not asking you to do anything about it. I just wish that I had a good excuse to give them. Most have only met you briefly. Some have only seen you at balls and simply wish the opportunity to talk with you. It's difficult to give them a reason as to why."

Ruth huffed, but didn't have an answer for him. She knew that 'she doesn't want to marry' wouldn't be taken as an acceptable answer. She would be expected to find a husband eventually. And eventually was approaching far sooner than she would like.

Ivy cleared her throat a little, finally seeming to have given up on staring at her tea cup. "I was just thinking," she ventured. "Why don't you tell them that she's already being courted?"

Thomas waved his hand dismissively. "They would ask who the suitor is. It would be difficult to invent and maintain the illusion of an imaginary man."

"Well, aren't you already doing that? With The Owl, I mean."

"Yes, and look how well that's turning out."

Ruth shook her head, her fingers tapping on the table as she thought. "No, I think Ivy might have a point. I could just say that I'm involved with The Owl."

"But we're already having a problem with that little masquerade. Making it more complicated won't help matters."

"I don't see how it would make it worse," she countered.

Thomas stared, though Ruth knew that he wasn't truly looking at her. It was the look he had when he was processing a particularly extraordinary idea of hers. His mind needed time to catch up.

"No," he finally agreed. "I don't suppose it could possibly make it worse at this point, could it? Your mother most likely won't be happy with the falsehood, but I doubt she would go so far as to out you. However, this doesn't change the fact that The Owl doesn't exist."

"Apart from James' pestering, no one has seemed too dubious of our story that he is simply reclusive. With my own nature, most will probably think it's a good match."

"Well, quite. Though there will come a time when people will expect a wedding, and you cannot marry a man who does not exist."

"That is a problem for another day. If nothing else, we can say I broke it off when the lack of wedding becomes too conspicuous and hopefully, by that point, my age will lead to things calming down."

Ivy let out a small laugh. "I don't know any other woman who is so keen to age."

"Do not misunderstand me, Ivy, I do greatly appreciate my looks. I just wish everyone else would appreciate them a little less. Or do so from afar."

"Ah yes, how terribly inconvenient it must be to have such beauty."

Ruth knew that she was joking, but it still stung. "Don't be so glib," she said, in a tone she hoped was equally joking, instead of betraying the twisting of her insides. "I was simply being honest."

Ivy nodded, seemingly catching onto Ruth's discomfort.

"Anyway, we should head back to the workshop. We still have the eye problem to fix."

"The eye problem?" Thomas asked. "What eye problem?"

"Mech has none. His body won't get him far without any."

"That's not true," Ivy countered. "Old Guinevere, who lives down the street from me, has been blind since she was a little girl. Mum said it was illness. Almost killed her.

But Guinevere worked her whole life and has six grandchildren, so she must manage somehow."

"Hmm. Perhaps we'll hire this Guinevere to teach Mech how to get about without any sight if we can't figure out eyes for him."

Thomas frowned. "Surely, you can use cameras of some kind?"

"Cameras are not swift," Ruth reminded him. "Nor are they particularly compact. These need to fit in his head."

"Well how do Fralsens see to drive?"

"They don't. They have an inbuilt map of London and all road users have little transmitters which alert the Fralsens to their proximity. Anything more complex than that is beyond us."

"Fair enough. I shall leave that to you. But a blind mechanical man will be difficult to sell."

"My job is to create," Ruth reminded him. "Yours is to figure out how to sell the creations. If I try to think about profitability, it will clutter my thoughts."

Thomas rolled his eyes. "Now you sound like an artist. A poor one at that."

"Then it's a good thing that we have no fear of starving, isn't it?"

9

"Yes, these will do nicely," Ruth said as she inspected the materials Ivy had collected for her. "Here, I have compiled another list of things I need."

Ivy gave an exasperated sigh, though she clamped her hand over her mouth just a moment later, as if shocked at her own impertinence.

"Sorry, Ruth," she squeaked. "I just... Why don't you come with me? Get some fresh air."

"Now you sound like Thomas," Ruth said as she folded her arms.

"Well, I mean... Maybe he has a point? You never leave the house unless he's dragging you to a ball."

"He and I have calculated every event I need to attend to appear sociable. Balls have more people of high standing attending than any other event, so attending them allows me more time between outings."

"You really hate leaving the house that much?"

"Yes," Ruth said, as if it was a completely obvious sentiment.

Ivy sighed. "I just... I... I don't mean to complain, but you're sending me out to pick up materials so often that it seems as if I barely see the inside of the workshop anymore."

"You're the only one I trust to get the things I need."

"I know, and I am thankful for that trust, but... I kind of feel more like a stooge than an apprentice."

Ruth sighed, frustration building. She didn't *have* anyone else to send to get the materials without messing it up. As it was, Ivy's arrival had solved a lot of problems for her when it came to material acquisition.

But, as she turned to Ivy to explain as much, she noted that the girl's fists were gripping her skirts so tightly that her knuckles had significantly paled. She wondered why she would be doing such a thing, looking her over for any other signs of distress. It took her a moment to realise that her jaw was firmly set, but her eyes were slightly wide. She was scared, but trying not to be.

Another few moments of consideration brought Ruth to the realisation that Ivy wasn't intentionally trying to complicate things for her. She was just trying to stand up for herself.

Ruth would have probably argued the point further if Thomas hadn't also critiqued her decision to use Ivy for every trip to purchase materials for her. He had been worried about Fralsen spies, though Ruth hadn't taken his concern seriously. Fralsen's attitude towards The Owl had always been to ignore him and hope that he went away. Ruth had once hoped to spur them into innovation, but that now seemed a lost cause.

Regardless, Thomas had worried that constantly having the same person making purchases on her behalf would make her easy for Fralsen spies to track. Ruth didn't believe that these spies existed, but if Ivy was also starting to tire of the trips...

"Fine. You may hire another person to go on these trips for you. See Thomas about the money. However, I will have nothing to do with it, I refuse to see this person, and you are still in charge of making sure that everything is exactly as I have asked for it. I refuse to work with sub-par materials."

Ivy nodded with a grin. "Of course. That's fine. I'll go and sort it out now."

Ruth gave a nod of consent, but still stopped Ivy just before she left the room. "I just wanted to say… I apologise if I am not all that you had hoped I would be as a mentor. I've not had a student before and, as you have possibly gathered, I do not know how to handle the company of others. You are a quick study, so I have opted to just leave you to your own devices, but if that's not enough…"

Ivy shrugged. "You talk when you work, and Thomas has been kind enough to provide me with money to get any books I want to teach myself. I'm catching up."

Ruth felt guilty at that. As much as Ivy said it was enough, she very much felt as if she was just trying to make Ruth feel better about her neglect.

"Perhaps I could take a look at one of those projects you have been working on," Ruth proposed. "I'll give you any assistance you need. Or just a critical eye, if you would prefer."

"Truly?"

Ruth shrugged. "There's nothing particularly pressing. Thomas probably won't be happy with me taking my time with building a body for Mech, but it's not the end of the world."

10

"Now, Mech, what do you see?" Ruth asked the metal skull resting on the table, which was now connected to a glowing blue tube that Thomas had acquired for them. An aether core. Ruth had been sure that she wouldn't get her hands on one for years, given their potential volatility, but now that it was in her hands, she felt no sense of danger, only wonder.

How quickly the world was changing before her very eyes. And her hands would help to sculpt it.

"You and Miss Ivy, I believe," Mech replied after a while. "Is that truly what humans look like?"

"I should think so, assuming you have not mistaken the table for us or anything like that. Or, at least, the well-endowed women look like this at any rate."

Ivy failed to hold back a surprised bark.

"What?" Ruth asked her.

"Nothing. I'm just not used to being referred to as 'well-endowed'. Especially not from a lady such as yourself."

Ruth rolled her eyes. "I was merely being factual. I have quite the womanly figure, but I think you have me beat. It's difficult to tell with the height difference. You are so much shorter than me."

Ivy glared at her, but her failure to contain her smile betrayed its facetious nature.

"Could you perhaps not move so much?" Mech asked them. "You have become a blur."

Ruth sighed. "Unfortunately, that is something you will have to get used to. I haven't yet managed to get the exposure time to what I want. It's only a few seconds but, if someone moves, you will see it as blurred, and you'll only get a new image once it's finished exposing."

"I shall endeavour to adjust."

"Thank you. Though I also lament your lack of depth perception. I have yet to figure out how to have you process two images to judge distance."

"I am sure I will manage," Mech assured her. "May I test my body now?"

"Not quite," Ruth told it. "The right shoulder is giving me a bit of bother. Give me until tomorrow to have it fixed up."

"Of course."

"I'll get you some more tea," Ivy said as she headed out of the door, only to come rushing back a moment later. "It's James! James is back."

Ruth nodded as they both hurried to get changed.

By the time Thomas had brought James up the stairs, they at least managed to look vaguely respectable.

"James," Ruth greeted. "This is a surprise. You have been quite scarce around here lately."

She hoped that her tone wasn't such that he thought she was making light of the fact that she had rejected him. She was very aware that that was the reason he hadn't been around.

"Well, I hadn't planned to be back so soon, if I'm being honest, but this situation with The Owl is getting a little bit ridiculous. I cannot extend a contract to someone I have not met. So, if he will not meet with me, I have an invitation from someone he cannot refuse."

"Someone he cannot refuse?" Ruth asked as James passed her the invitation.

"Here. I believe you are familiar enough with him to pass the message along for me," he said curtly before turning to leave.

Ruth rolled her eyes as soon as his back was to her. If he was going to be petty over her rejecting him, he could at least have the good graces to do it far from her presence.

Ivy escorted him out as Ruth turned her attention to the letter in hand.

She froze as she read.

Thomas frowned at her as she finished. "What did it say?"

"Queen Victoria has asked that The Owl attend a ball she is hosting," Ruth finally managed. "It seems she wishes to discuss his inventions in person."

Thomas paled. "It seems our bluff has been called. It will be impossible to lie our way out of this one."

"Is there truly nothing we can do? We could accept and then say he has the flu at the last moment."

"They are already suspicious. No, The Owl not attending will most likely end the deal and bring us increased scrutiny."

Ruth sighed, folding her arms. She didn't want to give up. She had been so aimless before she had found inventing, always feeling out of place in a world not built with her in mind. Inventing had given her a sense of purpose and this contract had been something to strive for. As much as she mocked Thomas using his money to keep score, she was doing the exact same thing.

Ruth wanted The Owl to be one of the greatest names of the age, and working for the Crown would certainly help her along the way.

Thomas sighed, folding his arms. "Perhaps we can hire an actor to pretend to be The Owl. Not that I know any, or would trust any to keep their mouths shut."

Ruth hummed in thought as she looked back towards the workshop, seeing Mech's head resting on the table through the slightly ajar door.

"I think I have a better idea," Ruth said before hurrying through to her workshop.

11

"This is never going to fool anyone," Thomas said with folded arms as he glared at Mech.

"It's going to work fine," Ruth said as she and Ivy finished covering his skeletal hands with gloves. Ruth had wanted more of a solid covering for him, but time was not on her side. And it wasn't as if anyone would see it anyway.

"How do I look?" Mech asked as Ruth and Ivy stepped back to admire their handiwork.

"Not bad," Ruth told him honestly.

His coat and trousers hung well over his metallic frame, making him very much appear as a man. The only thing giving him away was his head, which still very much looked like a metal skull.

"What about his head?" Thomas asked, echoing Ruth's thought process.

"We can cover it," Ruth figured as she moved over to the selection of wigs and masks she and Ivy had picked up.

"What could possibly cover him to the extent that will fool anyone?"

Ivy sighed at him as Ruth found a decent prospect.

"You're not being very sporting," she said as Ruth made her way back over to Mech.

"I'm sorry if I don't want to be caught lying to the Queen of England."

"You won't be," Ruth assured him. "Mech only has to get through this one ball. We don't even have to stay that long. He just has to be seen."

She pulled the wig and mask over Mech's head and adjusted them so that all of his metal parts were covered. His eyes still had an eerie and not altogether human quality about them, but she supposed that couldn't be helped.

"He can't wear a mask all of the time. And he looks ridiculous with every inch of his skin covered like that. Even your fashion sense cannot make that look reasonable."

"You could say he's foreign," Ivy figured.

"Yes!" Ruth agreed, bouncing a little with excitement at the idea. "The French always have ridiculous fashion sense."

"Does he speak French?" Thomas asked.

"No, but that will be easy enough to remedy. I taught him English, didn't I?"

"Yes, but you speak English. You do not speak French, or do you not remember your crying fits that had your tutor give up?"

"Je parle français," Ivy said.

"Pardon?"

"I speak French," she clarified.

Thomas' eyebrows shot into his hairline. "Where did you learn to speak French?"

"Sailors, mostly. Traders from across the channel. Hanging around the docks annoyed my mum and it was a good way to cure boredom. Every so often, when she was being too overbearing, I would threaten to abscond to Paris with some new lad. Always sent her into a rage."

"Used to?" Thomas asked, folding his arms.

Ivy shrugged. "When I started working here, I was suddenly in much less of a hurry to end up in trouble."

"Probably because Ruth provides more than enough trouble for anyone."

Ivy smiled. "Probably."

Thomas sighed, pinching the bridge of his nose between his fingers. Ever since Ruth had proposed her plan to have Mech pretend to be The Owl, he had been noticeably stressed. Even with her faith in her abilities, Ruth had to admit that she was struggling with sleep even more than usual.

If this failed, they would most definitely tarnish the family name beyond repair. It would be a scandal that even Ruth's mother, with all of her wit and charm, would be unable to recover from.

Mech, seemingly noticing their concerned thoughts, moved over to the two of them. His movements weren't as fluid as his flesh counterparts', but they were more than passable.

"Do you need a cup of tea?" Mech asked her.

Ruth gave a confused frown.

"Miss Ivy always makes you tea when you're upset."

Thomas raised an eyebrow. "He can read facial expressions now?"

"Ruth frowns when she's upset. It is not a difficult pattern to notice."

Ruth hummed in thought, her frown not leaving. Mech was supposed to simulate conversation. She had wired him to notice patterns in conversation in the hopes that he could learn and progress on his own, but she hadn't realised that could also be extended to facial expressions.

Ruth shook her head, deciding to refocus. As long as Mech was walking and talking, there wasn't a problem, and she needed to concentrate on the details to make sure he would convince people.

12

"Let's walk around the room one more time," Ruth said as she had her arm linked in Mech's. She could feel his joint beneath the fabric and had to be careful not to hurt herself, but that was far from her primary concern in that moment.

Mech still lacked proper depth perception, so Ruth was compensating by guiding him so that he didn't bump into anything. She had added tweaks to his outfit until it no longer looked so outrageous and used pieces of cream fabric to mimic skin in a couple of places, though not enough to draw attention to the fact that it didn't quite look right. His movements were still stiff, but not enough to cause someone's mind to jump to 'mechanical'.

In the end, Mech was a pretty believable facsimile for human.

Or, at least, he was as good at faking as Ruth was, which was close enough.

"He'll be fine," Ivy said as she walked into the room and Ruth did a double take as she saw that she was wearing the dress she had bought her.

"You're coming with us?"

She nodded. "As Thomas' guest."

"I thought you said you didn't want to go to balls."

"I don't, but if something goes wrong with Mech, Thomas will be useless. And I didn't exactly want to pass up an opportunity to see the Queen."

Ruth grinned. "Then let's go."

Ruth smiled as she heard Ivy gasp as they pulled up to Buckingham Palace. It was a particularly impressive sight, she had to admit. Enough to distract her from running through everything that could possibly go wrong during the night.

"It will be fine," Ivy assured her, noticing her frown. "Mech is more than up to the task, aren't you Mech?"

"Oui," the mechanical man replied with a convincing accent. At least, to Ruth's ears, which she had to admit weren't particularly attuned to such things.

"You'd better be," Thomas said, anxiously glaring out of the window, as was a habit of his.

Ruth focused on the feel of her corset tight around her middle to calm herself as the carriage stopped.

Mech stepped out first and Ruth held her breath, waiting for him to stumble on the step he couldn't see. Thankfully, he managed with only the slightest wobble.

He held his hand back to the carriage and Ruth took it, glad for his lack of skin. There was something far more comforting to his fabric-covered metal.

Thomas and Ivy followed them closely as Ruth focused on leading Mech up the path.

Thankfully, they had arrived at about the same time as a large number of other guests, so they formed a small crowd that was easy to get lost in as they entered the palace and made their way to the ballroom. Feeling invisible helped Ruth's anxiety considerably.

Of course, that feeling disappeared the moment they entered the room and were announced.

"The Owl and Lady Ruth Constance Chapelstone."

Ruth could have sworn that the room went silent as every eye turned to her and Mech. She found herself unable to breathe until people gradually turned back to their previous conversations.

She watched carefully and saw that there was barely a fraction of the same reaction to Thomas and Ivy, confirming that it had been entirely down to The Owl's mysterious reputation.

Thomas had warned her that The Owl being so recluse had only encouraged interest in Britain's Greatest Inventor.

"I have been waiting a long time to meet you, sir."

Ruth let out a sigh of relief as James approached, focusing in on him instead of the glances and whispers she could feel aimed her way. She wasn't quite ready for complete strangers.

Mech turned to him, though Ruth had to nudge him a little as he turn all of the way.

"You must be James," Mech said. "Thomas has told me much about you."

"And yet he has told me little about you. Half of the boys were convinced you were horribly disfigured. Though I suppose your mask doesn't dispute that."

Ruth glared at him. "You are being a tad rude, James."

"It's quite alright, dear," Mech said, reminding her that they were supposed to be pretending to be a couple.

She took a deep breath as she realised that she hadn't done anything to bring that into question; she had just forgotten that it was part of their story.

"This is the height of fashion in Paris right now," he told James.

"We're not in Paris now."

"Oui, but I have been a tad nostalgic for home."

James raised an eyebrow. "You're French?"

"He's English," Ruth said, remembering the story Thomas had come up with. "But his mother was French and she insisted that he attend boarding school in Paris. He only returned a few years ago."

James nodded, seemingly buying it.

"Sir," a young man in a uniform said as he hurriedly approached. "There has been an issue that needs your urgent attention."

"If you'll excuse me," James said before hurrying off with the boy.

"Well, that went well," Mech said, though Ruth was already cursing under her breath as James' sister saw them and made her way over.

"Lady Chapelstone," she greeted. "It's been a while since I saw you."

Ruth nodded. "I don't have the sturdiest disposition," she explained. "I don't often leave the house."

"Yes, Thomas has told us. It's such a shame. James was quite keen on getting better acquainted with you." She turned to Mech. "But, of course, you don't need attention from other men when you have one of your own."

"Owl, this is Lady Anne Holly," Ruth introduced.

"Owl?" Anne asked with a raised eyebrow. "Doesn't he have a name beyond that?"

Ruth froze, not quite believing that they hadn't thought of that.

"Michel," she blurted out as her brain finally unfroze. "His name is Michel."

Anne smiled, seemingly not picking up on Ruth's nervousness.

"I'm glad I had the opportunity to meet you, Michel. Everyone has been quite excited about having the chance to meet the enigmatic mind behind some of the greatest inventions of the last few years."

"Thank you," Mech said, allowing Ruth to breathe a sigh of relief.

She was worried that he might make a social slip-up.

"Your hair ornament is quite fetching," he continued.

Ruth froze. Where had that come from?

Anne blinked at the random comment, but didn't otherwise comment, to Ruth's relief.

"Thank you. It actually has this magnetic component that unclips."

She had already unclipped it to show him before Ruth could think of a reasonable objection.

As soon as the ornament was near him, it sped off to attach itself to Mech's chest.

"Oh! How odd," Anne exclaimed.

Mech moved to extract it before Ruth could get to it and his arm became glued to his chest as Ruth did her best to suppress the urge to groan.

"How is it attaching like that with no metal?" Anne asked as Ruth yanked the magnet away from him, wondering just how strong it was.

"I have no idea," Ruth said, with no clue what else to say as she gave Anne her ornament back.

Anne frowned, giving Mech an odd look, but otherwise not saying anything.

Ruth hoped that him being mechanical was too much of a leap for her.

"If you'll excuse us, we should catch up with Thomas," Ruth said before dragging Mech away.

"Put your arm back down," she said as she realised that he was holding it up against his chest.

"I can't," he told her. "I appears to be stuck."

Ruth tugged it down so that it was at his side before sighing. There was no way that wouldn't attract attention if she didn't fix it.

"His name is Michel," Ruth said under her breath as she made her way back to Thomas and Ivy.

"Who?" Ivy asked.

"The Owl. We forgot to give him a name."

"Have you had any trouble?" Thomas asked.

"Anne had a magnetic hair clip and now Mech's arm doesn't work."

"Michel's," Thomas corrected.

"Right, Michel's, though I don't think that was the most important part of that sentence."

"Can you fix it?"

"Maybe. I'll need somewhere out of the way to take a look."

Thomas frowned in thought. "If I disappear too it may draw suspicion, but for you to go with him alone without a chaperone…"

"Ivy can go with me."

"Fine, but be quick."

"I will," Ruth promised before heading off with Mech — Michel — and Ivy.

"Where do you want to do this?" Ivy asked.

"Somewhere private. Beyond that, I don't care."

Ivy nodded before heading straight out into the hall and around a corner to a cupboard.

"How did you know this was here?"

"You predicted trouble, so I kept an eye out. You're not exactly the most observant, so it seemed prudent to keep note of the area."

Ivy grabbed a small gas lamp from a table and passed it to Ruth so that she would have some light.

"I'll keep an eye out for you."

"Thank you," Ruth said before heading into the cupboard with Michel, placing the lamp onto the shelf.

"Let me have a look," Ruth said before hiking up her skirt to reveal the tools she had strapped around her thigh.

Michel used his other arm to hoist up the broken one so that Ruth could inspect it. She pushed his sleeve up to look at the metal joints beneath.

"It seems Anne's magnet shifted a part of your elbow out of alignment. I should be able to get it back into place easily enough."

She got to work as quickly as she could.

She had barely started when there was a knock on the door.

"I'm not done yet," she said, as quietly as she thought would still carry through the door.

"You are Miss Ivy, correct?" Ruth heard through the door, identifying James' voice.

"That is correct, sir."

"What are you doing loitering in this corridor?"

"I just needed a moment to myself. This is my first ball and it's all a little hectic."

"Yes, I suppose that is what happens when someone like Thomas lets his tastes run a little… lower class."

Ruth riled up immediately, but knew that giving away her presence would do nothing to help. She redoubled her efforts on Michel in the hope that they could leave the cupboard as soon as James turned his back so that she could comfort Ivy if she needed it.

"Maybe Thomas is just tired of all you aristocrats and your out-of-touch ways."

Ruth held back a snort at that.

"Just because he wants something exotic for now doesn't mean that he will still want it when it comes time to settle down."

"Careful, sir. One might think your concern stemmed from a *personal* interest."

Ruth frowned. What had Ivy meant by that?

She heard James splutter. "How dare you insinuate something of that nature."

Of what nature? Ruth thought to herself as she finished aligning Michel's elbow, only for a stray bolt to fall to the floor with a loud clang.

"What was that?" she heard James ask.

"Nothing," Ivy said quickly.

Ruth cursed under her breath as she tried to figure out how to cover up what they had been really doing. After a moment, she came to the only logical conclusion and pulled Michel's sleeve down over his exposed joints before ruffling his shirt.

"What are you doing?" Michel asked lowly as she tugged at her corset.

"Hopefully only tarnishing James' idea of me, not my entire reputation."

She moved into Michel's arms as James yanked the door open, despite Ivy's protests.

"James!" Ruth exclaimed as she extracted herself from Michel. "We were just…"

James became immediately flushed. "Ruth! This is highly inappropriate. You two aren't even betrothed."

"Actually they are," Ivy said quickly. "He proposed just before we got here. You can forgive them their excitement, I'm sure. Unless, of course, you want me to tell Thomas who *you* want to get excited with."

James spluttered before silently nodding.

Ruth and Michel followed Ivy back through to ballroom.

"What did you mean by that?" Ruth asked Ivy.

The younger woman smirked. "Much like me, James isn't very discriminatory when it comes to the gender of his partners. Of course, given his position, he is a lot more careful with the information. The real shame is that Thomas feels the same way, but they'll never get over their need to protect their images."

Ruth frowned. "Wait, Thomas feels the same way? But I thought… You and Thomas seemed to be getting closer."

Ivy snorted. "No, Ruth, Thomas is definitely not interested in women."

Ruth blinked. "Oh. I hadn't realised. If I had, I would not have made an assumption about your relationship."

Ivy frowned. "How did you not know? He has never been subtle about it. In fact, I'm sure I've heard him outright refer to his preference in your presence at least twice in the past week."

Ruth simply blinked again. "I had not noticed. If I am being honest, I tend to stop listening when you two discuss social matters."

Ivy smiled, shaking her head. "Regardless, I'm just here to help you out and to keep your uncle's reputation in good standing. Rumours start spreading if you go so long without a companion at social events, as I'm sure you would have learned if not for Michel."

"Yes. Who I am now apparently engaged to."

"I'm sorry, but I had to think on my feet. That seemed like the best way to do it."

Anne spotted them at that point, approaching quickly.

"Ruth! Did you hear? James came back for just a moment before saying that there was an emergency the Queen had to attend to." She turned to Michel. "It looks like you won't get to meet her after all."

"It's alright," Michel assured her. "I mostly came because my not having met James yet was becoming a security issue. Now that we have met, Thomas should be able to negotiate my contract with the Crown."

Ruth smiled. "If you don't mind, Anne, we should be heading home. I don't do well with staying awake too late."

As soon as they returned to the house, Ruth was bouncing up and down with excitement.

"Did you see that? We did it! James saw The Owl and no one figured out he wasn't real."

Thomas sighed, folding his arms. "Yes, except now you're engaged to him. That's not going to end well."

"Oh, lighten up," Ivy said with a grin. "Now, if you'll excuse me, I have to figure out how to extract myself from this cumbersome mess." She pulled at her skirts.

"They aren't that bad," Ruth defended.

"Yes they are," Ivy shouted back as she headed out of the room.

Ruth grinned as she offered Michel her arm. "Come on," she said to the mechanical man. "You've been running all day. We should shut you off and make sure everything is still working."

"Of course, my lady," Michel said, taking her arm.

13

Ruth smiled as she sat back on her chair in the workshop, refining Michel's new arms. They had better covering, which looked far more like their human counterparts, though they had a bit of intricate detailing because Ruth couldn't resist, even though she knew no one was going to see them.

James was downstairs negotiating with Thomas, and Ruth was glad that he was no longer chasing after her. Ivy assured her that James had originally had feelings for both her and Thomas and her unavailability had shifted all of his focus to Thomas. She was downstairs serving them tea, mostly because she found it amusing to watch them blush around each other.

"Do you think we should go downstairs and see what they're talking about?" Ruth asked, having reached a nice break in her work. "They are, after all, discussing my inventions."

"That does sound like a good idea," Michel agreed, though Ruth knew it was just because he was programmed to agree with her.

"I'll just get changed and we can head down."

As soon as she had a clean dress on, Michel accompanied her downstairs to where Thomas and James were talking.

"This is truly a work of genius," Ruth heard James say and couldn't help but grin as she and and Michel approached.

"You boys admiring The Owl's new invention?" Ruth asked and she and Michel entered the room.

Thomas stiffened a bit but she didn't notice as James was pouring over her plans.

"Admiring? This could revolutionise the Empire!" James exclaimed. "A mechanical soldier... Amazing!"

Ruth froze dead as she identified the plans on the table as the ones for Michel.

"Soldier?" she eventually managed. "It's not a soldier, it's... It's... Well, anything else."

James gave her an odd look and she realised that, as far as he was concerned, she had no authority on the matter.

She turned to Michel. "Tell them. It's not a soldier design."

"It's not a soldier design," he repeated.

James turned back to Thomas. "If you sell us it, we will use it as a soldier. Think of all of the lives we can spare. All those soldiers who no longer have to die."

"And what about those on the other side, fighting soldiers who are so easily replaced?" Ruth demanded.

"Enemies of the Empire."

"Human beings!"

"Alright," Thomas said loudly as he stood up. "I have a policy against politics in my house. James, I will be in touch about these designs and about finalising Michel's contract with The Crown."

James nodded before leaving.

As soon as Thomas had finished seeing him out, he headed back to where Ruth and Michel were waiting.

"You cannot sell my designs as weapons," she protested, her hands on her hips.

"What did you think I was selling them as? Why do you think the Crown was so interested?"

She drew up short at that. She hadn't really thought about what happened to her designs once Thomas sold them. She hadn't thought of any of them as weapons but, the more she thought about it, she realised that many had military applications.

Thomas sighed, shaking his head. "Why do you care? If these things are going to exist, better that they're in Queen Victoria's hands."

Ruth felt a sting behind her eyes as she tried to fit the idea of her inventions being sold as weapons with her idea of them. As far as she was concerned, she was an artist who used metal instead of a canvas. Her inventions were about making the world a better place for people, not killing them. She had originally designed the parts for Michel to help people who had lost limbs, and now Thomas wanted to sell them as weapons that would probably take more.

"They were never meant to be weapons."

"Intent doesn't matter, Ruth. If they have military applications, someone will use them. As I said, better that it's Queen Victoria."

"No. Better that it's no one." Ruth turned to Michel. "Come on, let's go pack."

"Pack?" Thomas asked.

"If you're selling my designs as weapons, then I won't design any more. I'll go home."

Thomas sighed. "Fine," he said as she reached the stairs. "I'll try to alter the deal with the Queen. Lord knows how I'll do it, but I will figure it out."

Ruth smiled. "Thank you."

14

Ruth fidgeted with one of her favourite dresses. It had just the barest ornamentation, and she thought that it helped to sharpen her features, making her seem more formidable.

Thomas had arranged another meeting with James to talk over the terms of Ruth's contract with the Crown. Ruth hoped to add clauses to stipulate that none of her inventions would be used by the military, but Thomas had warned her that it would be unlikely. He thought it more likely that there would be conditions put in place to outline exactly which circumstances her inventions could be used in, many of which would favour the Crown over Ruth. But she was determined to get as much as she could.

She took Michel's arm and headed downstairs as she heard a knock on the door. She had talked over most of her ideas for what she wanted with Michel, but also knew that he would back her up with whatever she said in the meeting.

"Ruth, Michel," James greeted coldly as he entered.

"If you'll follow me," Ivy said, leading them through to the room Thomas usually used for his business meetings.

"Is it really necessary for your fiance to sit in on this meeting?" James asked.

Michel, thankfully, repeated back the words Ruth had taught him. "Ruth is my muse. It would be bad luck not to have her with me."

Ruth was pretty sure she heard James mutter "French men," under his breath like a swear. Or maybe it had actually been a swear. She was too far away to tell for certain.

They sat down around the table as they entered the room, but James didn't follow them.

"It's time to stop playing games," James said as he loomed over the others before dropping a bolt onto the table.

The bolt that had fallen from Michel back at the palace. Ruth had forgotten to pick it back up.

"It's a spare bolt," she noted, hoping that her tone was level. "Why are you dropping it on our table?"

"It wasn't difficult to figure out your little ruse, especially after I saw the designs for a mechanical man." He moved over to Michel before ripping off his wig and mask, showing the metal skull beneath.

"The Owl isn't real. He never was." James turned to Ruth. "It was you all along, wasn't it? There is no reason for Thomas to hide behind the persona, and you only brought Ivy onto your staff when you arrived in London, long after The Owl had started working."

"James, that's enough," Thomas said. "What do you want?"

"I want The Owl," he glared at Ruth, "to sign the contract to work with the Crown, as it is, and to abide by it."

"And if I don't?" Ruth asked, folding her arms.

"If you don't, I will make your ruse public. Lying to a representative of the Crown in such a way could be enough for prosecution, not to mention the hit your reputation would take. Not only have you made a persona so that you could pursue activities unbefitting a woman of your station, but you have built yourself a metal husband. What scandalous tastes you must have to find him a suitable bedmate."

Ruth turned bright red as she stood up. "That is enough! I built Michel so that I would not have to marry a brute like you."

"But that's not what people will say," James said, smirking, and she had to admit that he was right.

"The contract is for me to build weapons, correct?"

"Indeed."

Ruth sighed. She didn't want to sign it, but she truly had no choice.

"Ruth, you don't have to," Thomas said.

She shook her head. "I will not ruin the family over this. My tendencies towards Icarus-like behaviour got me into this situation. It's only fair that I am the one to pay for it."

She leaned down to sign the contract that James placed in front of her. The pen felt heavy in her hand and her signature was shakier than usual. She signed as The Owl, since she doubted James would be the only one to see the document. She trusted him to keep her secret, otherwise he would lose his leverage over her, but she didn't trust anyone else.

"There you go. You have your damn contract. I hope you're happy with yourself."

"I have done my duty to the country," James said simply. "I just wish you understood that."

"I understand just fine. I just don't like seeing my designs perverted."

"If you never thought that was a possibility then it is time for you to grow up." James took the contract at that and headed to the door.

As soon as it shut behind him, Ruth slumped back down into her chair, feeling utterly defeated.

"What now?" Ivy asked her, finally stepping forward from the corner where she had been lurking.

"Now I do as he says," Ruth said with a sigh. "He's right. If he outs me, it will shame the whole family. That's not something we can risk."

Ivy sighed. "So you're really going to do it? Build weapons?"

"I'm going to keep building what I've always built. If someone finds a way to use them as weapons… I suppose it's out of my hands."

"They're still your inventions," Ivy protested, though her voice was weak. It was obvious that she understood that fighting was futile.

"I know," Ruth said. "But there's nothing I can do, and I would very much like to try to sleep at night."

15

"Ivy, I need more tea," Ruth said as she finished the final touches on her latest upgrade for Michel.

"Ivy isn't here," Michel told her, prompting her to spin around.

He was standing in the doorway — she hadn't even noticed he had left the room — holding a tray with pot of tea and some sandwiches.

"It is the middle of the night," he reminded her as he place the tray down. "She went home hours ago."

"You're right, of course," Ruth muttered as she returned to her work.

"I thought, given your recent tendency to work through the night, I would pick up her duties after she left. Of course, if you also slept through the day, I would suggest switching her hours to match yours, but your sleep hours are sporadic and short lived."

Ruth nodded in agreement, not lifting her focus from the work in front of her. Ever since she had signed the damn contract, she had struggled to sleep through the constant anxious nausea. Her brain refused to stop working, so she only slept when she passed out, slumped over her desk. Even then, it was only ever for a few hours at a time.

"Thomas worries that you will make yourself ill," Michel told her as he passed her a cup of tea.

She drank straight from the cup in gulps, forgetting about the temperature. Thankfully, Michel had anticipated that and had made sure to pass her a cup that had cooled enough not to burn her.

"If he has any advice for shutting my brain off, I would be happy to hear it. Besides a pistol, I mean."

Michel passed her a sandwich next. "You need to eat," he told her as she eyed it warily. Her stomach wasn't really up to food, but she honestly couldn't remember the last time she had eaten.

She reluctantly took the sandwich and nibbled at it.

Her stomach, in fact, seemed to settle at the reintroduction to food, so she made her way over to the tray to grab another one.

"Thomas has been busy with arranging the wedding now that everyone seems to be aware," Michel informed her.

"Oh," she said as she finished another sandwich. She hadn't really thought about the fact that pretending they were engaged would mean a wedding. "Why is he arranging it now? Surely it can wait."

"Technically, we live in the same house. It is seen as inappropriate and, apparently, James is doing all he can to fan those rumours. Thomas says that James thinks you won't go through with the wedding."

"He thinks I'll call it off and then what? Does he honestly believe I will let him court me after all he has done?"

"I asked Thomas about that. He says that James is just looking to make life miserable for you. Apparently choosing a mechanical man over him has been quite the bruise to his ego."

"I don't give a damn about his ego."

"That is perhaps the problem."

"Or maybe his fragility is the problem."

"That is a good point. I admit, I am still acclimatising to human interaction."

"As am I, and I have been at it a lot longer."

"Does it ever make any sense?"

"Not that I've found. You can occasionally find patterns, but as soon as you think you understand something, someone breaks from the norm and surprises you."

"How tiring that must be for someone who runs out of energy so quickly."

Ruth laughed a little, though it lacked real humour. "That's one way to put it." She reached for another sandwich. "So, this wedding: when is Thomas planning it for?"

"Well, there hasn't even been an event to officially announce our engagement. He's planning one for next week."

Ruth sighed. She really wasn't in a fit state for a social event, but at least Michel would be there to keep her company.

"Here," she said moving back to her workbench and taking the new upgrade from it.

She moved back to Michel before showing him the new covering, designed to fit around his metal skull. It didn't look human, being made up of interlocking white, ceramic parts, but it was still nicer to look at than his exposed metal joints.

"Keep still," she told him as she locked them into place over his face.

"How do I look?" he asked as she finally pulled away.

She smiled as she looked him over. "Less like something from a nightmare."

He moved his face plates oddly, and she realised after a moment that he was attempting to smile.

"Here," she said, passing him a mirror. "Have a look for yourself."

He shifted his face plates around, practising crude facial expressions. Ruth couldn't help but grin at his experimentation and curiosity.

She hadn't programmed him for curiosity, just to recognise the patterns around him in hopes that he would learn social skills. And yet, here he was, going out of his way to make sure she didn't starve in her stress.

"Thank you, Michel. For the tea and food. You're a good friend."

He looked up from the mirror and smiled once more, this time getting it right.

16

The day of the party came far too quickly for Ruth. Even spending her days in the void between sleep and wakefulness, as her mind refused to either rest or focus to its fullest extent, didn't slow down the inevitable.

She sighed as she fussed over her appearance once more in the mirror in front of her. She could hear the guests arriving downstairs and knew that she should be down there as well, celebrating her engagement, but the very thought exhausted her.

There was a knock at her door and she reluctantly turned away from the mirror, knowing that beyond the door was most likely someone who was there to drag her downstairs.

"Come in," she called.

The door opened and Michel stepped through, his clothing, mask and wig once more hiding the fact that he wasn't human.

"Thomas is wondering where you are," he told her.

She sighed, nodding. "I know. I just wish I didn't have to do this."

"Come on," Michel said, offering her his arm. "We can go downstairs and say hello to a few people as we make our way to the kitchen, where we'll hide for a while."

Ruth grinned at his plan, taking his arm. At least if she had Michel with her, it wouldn't be so bad.

Thomas greeted them as soon as they reached the bottom of the stairs.

"I'm glad you could finally make it down," he told her. "I was running out of excuses."

"I'm not feeling well," Ruth replied, her tone sharp. She had no idea how to soften it anymore.

He gave her a look she couldn't decipher. It was either disapproval or sympathy.

"She's down now," Michel said, and Ruth was thankful for not having to concentrate on her words. "We'll stay as long as she wants but, if she has to leave, I trust you can entertain the guests."

Thomas turned to Ruth with a bit of glare. "So now you're letting him speak for you?"

She shrugged. "Until he gets it wrong, yes." In the end, it didn't bother her because she had been the one to build and program him. He wasn't dictating her behaviour; he was saying the things she wished she could.

"Come on," Ruth said, steering him through towards the kitchen.

Anne quickly spotted them and headed over.

"Congratulations, Ruth," she said with a grin. "I'm glad that you've found someone, even if it's not someone of your station."

Michel responded before Ruth had a chance to. "Who needs titles when you have skills like mine?"

Anne's smile quirked a bit. "Well, I suppose that's true enough. Who knew that shy little Ruth would get along with someone so... confident."

"Opposites attract, as they say."

"I suppose they must if you two are getting along."

"If you'll excuse us, we have other guests to attend to," Michel said, moving away from Anne just in time for Ruth to fail at holding back her laugh.

"When did you get so confident?" she asked.

"I spent a lot of time trying to decide what kind of man The Owl should be. I talked it over with Thomas and Ivy, and we decided that a confident man, who was just a bit of a scoundrel, would make for a fine persona. Entertaining enough to distract from, well..." He trailed off, clearly aware of how many ears might be listening.

"Well, if you keep saying all of the things I am too polite to say, I am more than happy with it."

"Come on, let's try to slip away."

Ruth managed no more than an hour downstairs, even hiding as far from the crowds of well-wishers as she could. As soon as she saw the opportunity, she slipped away, back upstairs, though even there didn't feel safe. Anyone could wander up looking for her, after all. So, she climbed out of her window in the hope that no one would find her on the roof.

She sat down quickly in an attempt not to fall, her knees clutched to her chest, looking up at the airships travelling across the London night sky. She couldn't remember the last time she had felt so hollow. Her wedding was just a few days away, thanks to James' rumour mongering, and even inventing no longer gave her the escape she craved.

After a little while she heard a scraping noise behind her, and she spun around to see Michel climbing up to meet her on the roof.

"Michel, what are you doing up here? You might fall off."

"I could say the same to you," he countered as he came to sit down next to her.

She sighed into her skirt as she moved back to hugging her knees to her chest. "Maybe that would be best. If I just fell off this roof now, no one would be able to extort me. No weapons for anyone."

"And none of the good you do, either. No more replacement limbs. No more me."

"But at what cost, Michel? Every time I build something new, all I see are the ways in which it can be used by the military."

"Someone would have used them for such purposes eventually."

"I know. It's only… Maybe I was naive, but I didn't think about that. Not even for a second. I was so focused on the good I was doing, I couldn't see the harm."

"You are only giving them tools. How they use those tools is up to them."

"Then I should be careful about who I give my tools to." She sighed. "I have been over the arguments again and again, trying to find some peace, Michel. I simply can't."

"Then don't go through with the contract."

"I must. I can't ruin my family over this."

Michel fell silent at that, seemingly running out of arguments.

"What would you do?" Ruth eventually asked. "If you were me, what choice would you make?"

"I… I am only programmed for basic social interaction. This is quite beyond those parameters."

Ruth gave a sad smile. She had almost forgotten that, at the end of the day, Michel wasn't real. She had taught him how to walk and talk like a person, but she hadn't taught him how to be one.

"That's okay," she eventually told him. "I think it's beyond my parameters too."

She stood up, careful not to clip on the tiles, before offering her hand to help up Michel.

"I will do what I have to," she told him as he stood up. "I made this bed, so I guess I have to lie in it. No matter how many nameless people will pay for my mistake."

Michel didn't respond as she silently helped him back down from the roof.

17

Ivy sighed as she finished helping Ruth into her extravagant white dress.

Her wedding dress.

Every time she let herself think about the fact that she was about to be married, she felt her chest constrict with panic. She probably wouldn't have minded marrying Michel in order to secure her peace from others, but not like this. Not while she was being threatened with the truth and forced to pervert her creations.

Marrying Michel felt like committing to making weapons, as much as signing the contract had, if not more. At least signing the contract had only lasted a moment. The wedding was a day for her to wallow in her choice.

"You don't seem happy," Ivy said as Ruth spun in front of the mirror to get a better look at her dress.

At least she looked good.

"No, I suppose I don't," Ruth agreed as she examined her tired face in the mirror.

"You're supposed to be happy on your wedding day," Ivy told her. "My mother always said, if nothing else, when it comes to choosing a man, make sure that you're happy on your wedding day. If you're not, then it's not worth it."

"I guess that sounds like good advice."

"I guess it does, but Michel's not the problem, is he?"

Ruth snorted. "How could he be? I built him to be everything I need out of a husband; a friend and a mask for me to hide behind. I would always have independence while married to Michel, but not while James holds a noose around my neck."

Ivy gave her a sympathetic smile, but didn't have anything more to say. There was no answer. The situation simply was what it was.

"They're waiting for you," Ivy said after a while, reminding Ruth that everyone was waiting in the main part of the church.

Ruth nodded before following Ivy out of the room, to where Thomas was waiting for her. Her parents hadn't been able to organise coming down to London to see her married, which didn't really surprise her. They knew that Ruth had been The Owl all along, so they must have known that her marrying him was just a ruse. She doubted her mother approved, no matter what she thought the situation was. She definitely wouldn't if she knew the truth.

With her parents absent, Thomas was the one who had the job of walking her down the aisle.

"How are you feeling?" Thomas asked her.

"Like someone who has been forced into making a terrible mistake," she said, completely devoid of the inflection that should have indicated that her words were intended as a joke.

Thomas didn't try to lie, telling her that she had other options, and she was grateful for that as he offered his arm out to her.

She took it and focused on keeping her breathing steady as she walked forward.

The doors in front of her opened to show a sea of faces she didn't recognise. She didn't know any of these people, and she assumed that they were all acquaintances of Thomas.

In the centre of it all stood Michel in impeccable dress, waiting for her.

She focused on him and blocked out everything else.

He was her greatest creation and, even if no one else knew it, he was the thing she was proudest of.

And now James had the plans for him. More would be built and Michel's siblings would become machines of war. Expendable soldiers that could easily overwhelm an enemy with no loss of human life for the Empire.

How efficiently brutal they would be.

She almost didn't realise that they had reached the end of the line.

Thomas detached his arm from hers and left her facing Michel.

Her prototype friend-turned-soldier-turned-husband.

"Can we have just a moment?" he said to the priest, surprising her. What was he up to?

The priest looked surprised, but Michel ignored that as he stepped closer to Ruth.

"What is it?" she asked, very aware of everyone watching them with curiosity.

"You asked me a few days ago what I would do in your position and I just now figured it out."

"Michel-"

"Ruth, please. You can't go through with this. I wouldn't."

She blinked, surprised.

"I thought making that decision was outside your parameters," she eventually managed.

"So did I. I guess I'm more flexible than either of us thought."

"I suppose so," she managed.

Her friend-turned-soldier-turned-husband.

Turned-person.

If Michel was operating outside of his parameters, so might any others made from his designs.

They were people, and they were going to be used as expendable cannon fodder.

"If I don't, James will tell everyone. My whole family will be ruined."

Michel took her hands in his gloved ones. "Then tell them first." He nodded to the crowd in front of them, telling her exactly what he meant. "Tell them how you are such a great inventor that you built a person. That their rules made you hide behind your creation, but no more. They will understand. You are, after all, the Greatest Inventor in Britain."

Ruth nodded, realising that he was right.

She didn't have to play by James' rules.

"You truly are the greatest thing I ever created," she told him.

"Then let's show them."

She took a deep breath before turning to face the crowd staring at her with confused frowns.

"I'm afraid I have not been honest," she said clearly, her voice echoing around the empty room. "There is no Owl. There never was."

She reached up to Michel's face and removed his wig and mask, revealing the ceramic face beneath.

The room echoed with gasps. Ruth could have sworn that she saw someone faint out of the corner of her eye.

"Inventing was never seen as a suitable pastime for a lady of my station. My uncle created The Owl so that he could sell my inventions while I retained anonymity.

"However, after arriving in London, I realised that would no longer do. People wanted to meet The Owl, and I was being pursued by numerous suitors, despite the fact that I have never wanted to marry.

"In order to retain my independence and appease those who wanted to meet The Owl, I took to my workshop and built a man to pose as The Owl in my place. But no more. I cannot, in good conscience, keep lying."

She took another deep breath, completely unable to tell how the crowd in front of was reacting. Their silence gave away nothing.

"My name is Lady Ruth Constance Chapelstone, and *I* am The Owl. *I* am Britain's Greatest Inventor. I built a walking, talking, thinking man out of metal. If you can't see past my gender and station to appreciate that, then that is your problem, not mine."

She turned back to Michel.

"Come on," she said. "I think it's time for me to return home to my workshop."

As soon as Ruth had finished running the few streets back home with Michel in tow, she promptly threw up as the weight of what she had done finally hit her.

She had admitted to being The Owl.

And to building a metal husband.

Would they believe her?

Or would they think that she had made him to satisfy an odd bedroom preference?

She leaned back against the hallway wall as soon as the door closed behind her. She slid to the floor and started to cry.

She had no idea what else to do.

The tears seemed the only sensible thing left.

She waited and waited for Thomas or Ivy to return home.

Michel waited patiently with her as she blubbed in the silence of the house.

Neither Thomas nor Ivy came back. She assumed they were dealing with the mess she had made.

She had no idea how much time had passed when the knock at the door came, only that the room was bathed in the pink glow of sunset.

She wiped away her tears, along with a significant portion of makeup, before answering the door.

She presumably looked like something out of a nightmare, with her smeared face and her wedding dress worn from her run home. The knocker, however, remained stoic as he stood in full military attire.

"I have been sent to fetch you for the Queen," he told her.

Of course, she thought. She had just publicly announced that she had tried to dupe the Queen. That she had succeeded, really.

She nodded, knowing that fighting would do no good. They were most likely authorised to use force to drag her there if she protested.

"Your mechanical man too," the man at the door said.

Before she could protest, Michel was at her side.

"Lead on," Michel said to the man and Ruth smiled a little, glad that he was by her side.

18

The carriage ride to the palace seemed shorter than Ruth had remembered, though she supposed her dread might have had something to do with it.

The man from the door, who still hadn't properly introduced himself, led them inside as they arrived, taking them to a room they hadn't visited during the ball.

As he opened the door, she was greeted by the sight of Queen Victoria, regaled in black, sitting atop her throne and glaring down at her.

Ruth stepped forward, feeling incredibly silly in her tattered wedding dress, with her smeared face and wild hair.

"So," the Queen said, sitting even straighter, which Ruth wouldn't have thought possible.

Ruth felt herself wither under her stare.

"You are The Owl?"

"I... Yes, Your Majesty," she managed, her voice coming out as barely more than a whisper.

"I spoke with James. He was in charge of your contract, was he not?"

"He was."

"He told me that you had rejected the idea of your inventions being used in battle. He admitted to extorting you." She stood up and began to walk down to Ruth, not taking her eyes off of her. "I want you to understand that he did not have my leave to take such actions. He was acting entirely on his own, and he will be punished for such poor behaviour."

Ruth frowned a little, not quite believing what she was hearing.

"This is the metal man?" the Queen asked, indicating to Michel.

"Yes," Ruth managed. "I only intended to program him for basic social interactions, but he has since shown that he is capable of operating outside of his parameters. I can't think of a better threshold by which to judge humanity."

"Me neither," the Queen agreed as she examined Michel.

"Then please, Ma'am, you cannot build soldiers to his specifications. They would be no better than slaves."

"I quite agree," she replied as she returned her attention to Ruth. "And such behaviour is the domain of the Americans, not the British Empire."

"I thought they had stopped that after the war."

The Queen waved her hand dismissively. "Nonetheless, James was short-sighted. While your inventions are effective weapons, there are other ways for them to serve the Empire and I doubt putting you under duress would help the creative spirit. I would much rather have you working with us willingly."

"I... Really? Even though I'm a woman?"

"My dear, what gender do you think me to be?"

"Yes, but you're the *Queen*."

"And you are *The Owl*. Britain's Greatest Inventor. I will not allow such inconsequential things to stop the progress you could bring to the Empire."

"Thank you," Ruth managed.

"Now, Lady Chapelstone, I wish to bestow upon you the honour of the title of Crown Inventor. Will you accept?"

"Yes, Ma'am. I most certainly will."

L.C. Mawson

BOOK TWO

LADY RUTH AND THE PARISIAN THIEF

1

"There, I believe it's finished," Ruth said as she stood back from her workbench.

Michel and Ivy stepped forward to get a better look.

"It's so… *small*," Ivy commented.

"I believe that is the point," Michel replied.

"But does it work?"

Ruth rolled her eyes. "Oh ye of little faith," she said before pressing the button atop the mechanical spider.

It immediately started scuttling around the table, taking stock of its environment.

"Well, I suppose now we know that the smaller aether core prototype works," Michel commented.

"Yes," Ruth agreed. "Though now it's a case of scaling up my projects to see how powerful the smaller one truly is."

"So, what does this contraption actually do?" Ivy asked, folding her arms. "Besides look disconcertingly like a real spider?"

Ruth sighed. "It can do anything you need it to."

"Which will probably be espionage," Michel ventured.

Ivy frowned. "I thought you didn't want any of your inventions being used by the military."

Ruth shrugged. "I'm not particularly fond of the idea, but I can live with them being used for information gathering. Though, I had thought of them as more of a tool. You know, to get into those difficult to reach spots in engines and the like."

"Well, I suppose the strength of your inventions is their versatility."

"Is that a compliment for you or me?" Michel joked, his ceramic face plates quirking up into a little smirk.

"Both, I think," Ruth told him with a smile before turning back to Ivy. "And what about you? How is your navigational system coming along?"

"Nothing is currently on fire, so that's a good thing. Probably."

They heard a knock on the door downstairs.

"That will be your ride," Ivy said. "I'll let them in while you clean up."

Ruth nodded as Ivy left the room, quickly looking over herself in the mirror she had taken to keeping there so that Michel could practice facial expressions.

Her dark hair was falling out of its clip into a ruffled mess over her pale skin, framing her dark eyes as much as the red marks from her goggles. She had taken to wearing fewer skirts through necessity. With the three of them in the workshop at all times, they mostly just got in the way, not to mention the fire hazard. Her dress that day was a sky blue colour, which was only saved from stains by her leather apron. She had been careful, knowing that the Queen would most likely send for her. She hadn't wanted to change before seeing her.

Once Ruth had made sure that she looked at least vaguely presentable, she lowered her hand to the workbench, allowing the mechanical spider to climb up her arm.

"My Lady," the young man at the door - Peter, she remembered - greeted as she made her way downstairs. "Queen Victoria wishes to see you."

"I thought she would," Ruth said. Her meetings with the Queen, to go over how Ruth was faring as the Crown's Inventor and to see what uses her newest inventions might have, had never been explicitly scheduled, but it had quickly become clear that the meetings were always on the first of the month. "Let's head off then."

Ruth spent the carriage ride over to the palace looking over the little mechanical spider in her hands, considering different ways in which she could improve upon the design. It helped her to forget the bumpy road beneath her, though she found a headache forming as the carriage stopped.

She had never been good with travel.

Peter jumped out to open the door for her, as he always did. She waited patiently, knowing that it was polite, even if it would have quicker for her to open the door herself.

"Thank you, Peter," she said as she climbed down, the little spider climbing up to her shoulder to free up her hands.

Peter walked with her to where Queen Victoria was waiting. Ruth was used to the Queen's cold glares at this point, but the one she found herself under as she entered the room was particularly frosty.

"Ma'am?" Ruth asked, feeling a little on edge.

"I have just received word from our French ambassador."

Ruth blinked at the pregnant pause. "About?" she eventually asked, wondering what was going on.

"Mechanical men, apparently. Much like your Michel. The word around Paris is that they have been wandering the streets." The Queen gave her a measuring look. "No one else has even been close to developing mechanical men, as far as my intelligence tells me. Now, I will only ask you this once: have you sold or given the plans for Michel to anyone else?"

"No-" Ruth started, but cut herself off. "James got a look at the plans before I locked them away. But he can't have had that good of a look at them. And he was never the most mechanically minded individual."

"Locked away?"

"In Thomas' safe. He always kept my plans there until he could sell them. Not that he had any intention of selling the plans for Michel to anyone but James, but that was the first time he didn't intend to sell them."

"And the plans are definitely still there?"

"I... I don't know. We haven't had the need to put anything in the safe since I started working for you."

"You went home to Newcastle for a week two months ago. Have you checked the safe since then?"

"I don't know. Thomas might have."

"Then Peter will return to your home and check."

The wait for Peter to check the safe was excruciating. The Queen mostly ignored Ruth, focusing on her other work instead, but Ruth still felt as if she was taking up far too much space. Her discomfort certainly wasn't helped by her feeling the guards' eyes on her.

When Peter finally returned, it was with Michel in tow.

"Ruth?" he asked as he approached. "What's going on? Peter said that someone was building more mechanical men like me."

She nodded, feeling much better now that he was here, but didn't have a chance to answer before Peter spoke.

"Your Majesty, the safe was empty when we got there. It showed signs of tampering."

The Queen nodded before turning to face Ruth. "I want to believe that you were not involved in this, but what I believe isn't quite relevant right now. It is important that we shut down this operation, whatever it is, as quickly as possible and retrieve your plans. I can't send an occupation force to France, only a few of my best people. They will be most likely to succeed if you are with them. If you can help them to retrieve the plans and stop the production of these mechanical men, then we shall forget that this incident ever occurred."

"You would let her leave the country?" Michel asked, a little disbelieving.

"Under the watch of Captain Hall, yes. I trust him not to let her out of his sight."

"Then I'll do it," Ruth agreed. "I'll find the plans and stop whoever is creating more mechanical men."

2

"I'm coming with you," Thomas insisted as Ruth packed her things.

"And me," Ivy agreed.

"I had thought that my going was a given," Michel added, seeming a little thrown by what he was supposed to add to the conversation.

Ruth was too busy hurriedly - and badly - folding her skirts to tell him that contribution wasn't necessary.

"Ruth, I'm being serious," Thomas said, ignoring the others. "You cannot go to Paris alone. You know that you can't."

"I wouldn't be alone," she bit back, riling at his underestimation of her. "The Queen is sending me with one of her best captains." She declined to mention that Captain Hall was mostly there to make sure she didn't try to hide abroad.

"Well, I'm going with you," Ivy said. "I've never been abroad before and I have always wanted to see Paris."

Ruth couldn't help but smile at that. At least Ivy wasn't trying to chaperone her. "Well, far be it from me to stand in front of your dream," Ruth said as she finished packing her clothes, closing her suitcase.

"I am going as well," Michel told her. "These mechanical men - however they have been created - are like me. They are, for all intents and purposes, my siblings. I can't think of a better reason to be there."

"I had assumed you would want to come," Ruth assured him.

Thomas gave a frustrated sigh, folding his arms. "Your mother will kill me if I don't go with you."

"Then I shall mourn you with a heavy heart," she said, completely deadpan.

"That was sarcasm," Michel interjected, having only just recently mastered the concept.

"Yes, I am aware," Thomas told him before turning back to Ruth. "Please, Ruth. I was the one in charge of keeping the plans safe. I feel… responsible."

She nodded, finally accepting his reason. "You should all start packing if you wish to accompany me," she told them. "Peter is taking us to Captain Hall's airship in an hour."

Thomas raised an eyebrow. "You in an airship? Dear Lord…"

The carriage journey to the airship alone had Ruth forming a headache, which did not bode well for the journey to Paris. The journey wouldn't actually be that long - technically, it was shorter than the trip to Newcastle - but Ruth had never travelled well and air travel always came with the possibility of turbulence.

"Lady Chapelstone, I assume?" a rather gruff looking man asked as he approached. By his uniform, Ruth assumed that he was Captain Hall. He had an Italian look about him, with dark hair, olive skin, and a rather pronounced nose. As she got a better look, she realised that he was younger than his scars made him look, not more than a few years older than Thomas at most.

"That's right," Ruth said.

"I'm Captain Hall," he greeted. "Her Majesty has briefed you on the mission, correct?"

"Get the plans back and stop whoever is manufacturing more mechanical men. That about sums it up as far as I'm aware."

"Well, yes, I suppose it does. I don't suppose you have any ideas on how to go about that?"

Ruth stopped up short as Michel stepped forward.

"That is perhaps best tackled once the stress of travelling is behind us," Michel said.

Ruth had come to rely on Michel to explain her needs when her anxiety stopped her from verbalising her thoughts. Thomas had taken a proto-version the role before, but Ruth had never implicitly trusted him to get it right. Possibly because he often didn't. Michel, on the other hand, was refreshingly free of expectation and presumptions. Ruth had never been strange to him because she had been the first human being he had encountered.

Ruth had started to wonder if Michel would want something else - something more - out of life, but she hadn't been sure how to approach it with him. Or, perhaps, she was too worried about what his answer may be.

She had broached the subject with Ivy, who had just laughed and made jokes about Ruth's baby flying the nest. Ruth bristled at that. Not least because part of Michel's original purpose had been to act as a puppet husband for her so that she had no risk of losing her independence, or having to entertain an unwanted man in her bed.

Captain Hall seemed a little unnerved as he looked over Michel. "So, you're the mechanical man."

"That is correct. Though, I tend to go by Michel. It's a little easier on the tongue, don't you think?"

"Well, yes, I suppose it is." Captain Hall turned back to Ruth, clearly uncomfortable talking to Michel. "If you and the others could board the ship, we'll take off shortly."

Ruth nodded. "Of course. Could some of your men help with our luggage? We wouldn't be sure where to put it."

"Of course."

Captain Hall offered them all a full tour of the ship as they began to take off, but Ruth declined. She had far too much to do and far too many things to consider. Namely, what exactly she was going to do once they reached Paris.

Captain Hall took her straight to her room, where she immediately began to set up her workshop tools. She had brought as many as she could feasibly travel with. Her only real qualification when it came to hunting down mechanical men was that they were based on her designs. She knew their workings inside and out, which meant that she could potentially fashion something to prey on weakness in their design. Not that her designs usually had weaknesses, but Michel's design was very much a prototype. Ruth had added to Michel over time, but she had never bothered to update her plans. If she never made another mechanical man, there was no need, she had thought.

Ruth started by trying to remember all of her original designs for Michel and writing them down, doing her best to weed out any improvements she had made since. She was only about halfway through when her door opened, revealing Michel and Ivy.

"How did the tour go?" Ruth asked them, not looking up from her work.

"The ship is amazing," Ivy gushed. "You should have seen it. I'm sure Captain Hall will give you a tour later on."

"What are you doing?" Michel asked as he looked at the plans. "Is this me?"

"Well, you when I first built you. It will probably be useful to have the designs that the thief is working from." Ruth finally looked up from her work, scanning the room. "Where's Thomas? Shouldn't he be here to accuse you of distracting me from my work?"

"He's still with Captain Hall. I think he is a tad infatuated," Ivy explained.

Michel frowned. Or, at least, the ceramic plates that made up his brow angled down in a way that approximated a frown. "'Infatuated'? How so?"

Ivy frowned before starting to grin. "Wait, has Ruth not explained romance to you?"

"I explained the concept of marriage when he was going to stand in as my husband," Ruth said with a hand wave. "Anything else seemed superfluous."

Ivy shook her head before turning back to Michel. "Humans like to be around other humans. Sometimes we like other people in a… Well, we…" Ivy trailed off as she lost her confidence on the topic, and Ruth got the distinct impression that she would be blushing if she had light skin.

"He is neither human nor anatomically correct. As I said, superfluous."

Michel folded his arms in response to that. "Ruth, I would still like to learn about human interaction."

Ruth sighed, lifting her head from her work. "Humans are usually compelled to find partners in order to fornicate, which produces children when the partners are a man and a woman. Some humans, like me, have neither the compulsion to find a partner nor to fornicate. Humans like Ivy have the compulsion with both men and women, and humans like Thomas only have the compulsion with their own gender. Generally, however, only partnering with the opposite gender is considered acceptable. So, as far as the wider world is concerned, Ivy, Thomas and I all have the compulsion to find a partner to fornicate with of the 'appropriate' gender, and the 'appropriate' gender only."

"So, as a mechanical man, I will not have this compulsion either?"

Ruth shrugged. "Honestly, I have no idea how you're sentient. You are so far away from your original parameters, I can't tell you where you will go from here. Only you can decide that. But, no, it was never in your parameters, and you currently lack any of the requisite parts."

"Requisite parts?"

"There is nothing in your trousers," Ivy interjected.

"My legs are in my trousers."

Ivy smiled. "We'll buy you an anatomy book when we get into the city."

Michel nodded, but he seemed distracted by the plans in front of Ruth. "If I was built to these same parameters and I'm sentient, what about these other mechanical men?" he eventually asked. "Are they like me?"

"I don't know. Maybe."

"Do you think they know that they are made from stolen designs? That they're working for a thief?"

Ivy moved to his side, placing what Ruth assumed was supposed to be a comforting hand on his arm. "If Ruth and I weren't your first interaction with the world - if it was someone else who had built you for some nefarious purpose - would you have been able to tell?"

"Probably not," he admitted. "I knew nothing about the world until you explained it. I still don't know as much as I would like. I only know the world from your perspectives. I suppose I am lucky that you are both such upstanding individuals."

Ivy snorted. "That is the first time anyone has ever said that about me."

"I think my upstanding status was ruined when I announced that I would rather work as an inventor than ever get married."

Michel managed to give a close approximation of an eyeroll, and Ruth grinned with pride as she thought of how long he must have practised to perfect it.

"Regardless of your reputations, you have both been good friends and mentors to me."

Ruth continued to smile. "I'm definitely sure no one has ever said that to me."

"If I haven't, then it's only because I forgot," Ivy quickly said. "Otherwise, I wouldn't have hung around for so long. Your uncle doesn't pay me that well."

Ruth laughed a little at that. "Well, quite."

The ship made a slight lurching motion that made Ruth's lunch want to evacuate.

"I'm assuming that means we have arrived," Ivy said brightly as she jumped towards the door.

Ruth nodded before following, using Michel to steady herself.

3

The bridge was impressively ornate, with dark wood panelling lining the walls and bronze instruments littering the room. Ruth had only the vaguest idea of what any of the instruments did, but she found her mind aching for the knowledge almost instantly. Ivy tended to focus her inventions towards navigation and aviation, so Ruth made a note to ask her about it later.

"Ah, I see you have decided to join us," Captain Hall said, drawing her attention. His tone raised her hackles.

"I was busy drawing up a replica of the plans the thief took," she said defensively.

"So that they can steal a second copy?"

"So that I can look for a weakness."

Michel stepped to her side at that. "I can assure you, Captain Hall, with my superior strength and weight, your men would struggle in a fight against me. Similarly, I can theoretically be hit by bullets with only a small chance of taking any real damage. If the thief is using mechanical men like me as guards, your traditional combat methods will be of little use."

Captain Hall made a grunting noise as he nodded, before turning back to Ruth. "This doesn't help if we can't find these mechanical men of yours."

"I'm afraid I'm not familiar enough with Paris to give you a starting point," she admitted, a little annoyed. Captain Hall clearly wasn't too impressed with her, and she suspected that he didn't trust her. He possibly even thought that she had sold the plans herself. She hated to admit to him that there were things she didn't know.

"What about the local bobbies?" Ivy asked. "Might they know?"

"We're a military group on foreign soil without permission," Thomas said. "Or, at least, I assume we're here without permission. If the French government knew that they had the plans so easily within reach, they would most likely take them for themselves."

"Your assessment of the situation is accurate," Captain Hall said before turning back to Ivy and Ruth. "No local officials can be involved."

"Which brings us back to square one," Ruth said, placing her hands on her hips.

"I may be able to help here," Thomas said. "I have spent some time in Paris and have some friends in the city."

"Friends are one thing, actually getting relevant information from them is another," Captain Hall pointed out. "I doubt the nobility down there will be up to date on most of the problems of the city."

"Who said my friends were nobility?" Thomas asked with a smirk before turning to Ruth. "You and I should head down alone. My friends won't like me bringing a troupe with me, not to mention the attention Michel will attract."

"Ruth, that's not a good idea," Michel said. "You won't have any protection. The thief could be after you."

"Michel's right," Ivy agreed.

Ruth shook her head. "They already have the plans. Going after me would only give me more information about who they are. Thomas knows the city; we'll be fine."

Michel and Ivy didn't look happy at that, both of them turning to Captain Hall to see if he had any objections.

"We need the information and I'd rather not spook your friend. Go alone, but I'll send some men just to wander the area in case there's trouble. Nothing too close or conspicuous."

"Thank you," Thomas said before gesturing for Ruth to follow him off the ship.

The streets of Paris, Ruth quickly found, were just as noisy and crowded as those in London. The smells were slightly different, but still overwhelming. Ruth focused on how her corset tightly hugged her middle in the hope of grounding herself.

"So, where are we going?" Ruth asked as she kept tightly to Thomas' side.

"To a little cafe run by an old friend. Do you remember Adam?"

"Of course." Adam had been a childhood friend of theirs, and one of the only childhood friends Ruth had ever made. They had stopped seeing as much of him once they reached their adolescence and soon learned that his mother had sent him away to boarding school abroad, telling their mother in confidence that he had been troubled.

"Well, she now goes by Abigail."

Ruth blinked, trying to figure out what he meant. "Why would he take a woman's name?"

"Because she is a woman."

"Oh…" Ruth still couldn't say that she understood, but it also wasn't relevant to the task at hand, so she left it alone. "So, how does Abigail know about the mechanical men?"

"Well, I don't know that she does. However, she does know that it's your design, so if anyone would have been keeping note of any rumours of mechanical men, it would be her. Not to mention, she's the only friend I can quickly locate, so she can tell me where the others are if she doesn't have any of the information we need."

"It's certainly a good thing that you became so well-connected on your trips here."

"Well, having unique tastes tends to put you into contact with a rather diverse crowd."

He led Ruth around the corner to a small cafe. The cafe in question was reasonably busy, but not so packed that Ruth struggled.

As they approached the counter, Ruth almost did a double take. She wouldn't have recognised the woman behind the counter, if not for the scar above her lip. She remembered when Adam - or was it retroactively Abigail? - had tripped in her garden, cutting open their face on a sharp rock.

"Thomas!" Abigail greeted with a smile as Ruth noted that she was wearing a dress that indicated only modest earnings. She wondered if her family had cut her off.

"Abigail, it's good to see you again."

"I didn't think you would be back in the city so soon." She turned to Ruth. "And you brought Ruth?" She seemed a little uncomfortable at that.

"Ruth has ended up in a spot of bother. We thought you might be able to help."

"Oh? Sent out of the country to avoid a scandal? Though, after almost marrying a mechanical man, I don't know what more you could do to your reputation."

"This is less a matter of reputation and more one of treason."

"Treason? Against the British Empire?"

"Suspected treason," Ruth interjected. "Someone has stolen my designs for a mechanical man and we've heard of rumours suggesting that mechanical men walk the streets of Paris."

Abigail's gaze darkened. "Yes, I've heard these rumours, though I haven't seen the men."

Thomas nodded. "Do you know of anyone who has?"

Abigail sighed, before eventually nodding. "You didn't hear this from me, but one of my customers says that she has seen them coming out of a factory in the city. She's told me how startlingly inhuman they are."

Ruth folded her arms. "Only because they're working from prototype designs."

Abigail smiled. "I imagine so," she said before turning to Thomas. "I have the address if you want it."

Thomas nodded. "We shall head there right away."

"Not before you've tried my coffee!" Abigail exclaimed, rushing back to a strange contraption behind the counter.

Ruth watched with fascination as she produced a dark brown liquid in a china cup. The smell was overpowering and she sipped at it cautiously.

She made a surprised chirp as she found that she quite enjoyed the taste. Not as much as tea, but it was far from objectionable. She finished her cup as quickly as possible without burning herself.

"Can I have another?" she asked as Thomas had barely started his.

"Of course you can," Abigail said with a smile.

Thomas glared at her. "You know that I'm the one who will pay for this later, don't you?"

"Of course."

4

Ruth felt as if the whole world had slowed down around her as she and Thomas finally left Abigail's. She was used to her mind racing ahead of everyone else's, but this was far more intense. As she babbled on at Thomas about her ideas for stopping any mechanical men they encountered, he took even longer than usual to respond, and she felt far more frustrated than usual at having to slow down to explain basic concepts to him.

"Ruth, are you sure you're feeling right in the head?"

"Of course," she told him. "Though, I suppose, my heart is racing a little."

"Yes, well, you're bad enough with just tea. Giving you coffee was never going to be a good idea."

"I am perfectly fine," she defended.

"You would say that," he muttered, before shaking his head. "What do you think we'll see in this factory?"

"I have no idea. I suppose we'll find out when we get there."

"Do you think we should head back to the ship and get someone to come with us? If we encounter any of these mechanical prototypes, Michel would be able to fight them on equal footing, and Captain Hall's men would at least be able to put up something of a fight."

"We're just going to have a look. If we see any mechanical men, we can easily head back to the ship. They're not going to attack two people in broad daylight."

"I suppose that would be foolish of them. Let us hope that whoever stole your plans was able to put them together with enough skill for these men to not be foolish."

"I would wager that they are more likely to be sensible than any human men we may encounter."

"You may be right."

Ruth found herself gravitating a little closer to Thomas as the streets got narrower and darker, the sunlight blocked by poorly stacked buildings.

They approached the factory Abigail had directed them to and found that it was decrepit, with many of the windows smashed and the paint on the doors peeling.

"It doesn't look like anyone has been here in years," Ruth commented as she examined the broken windows.

"No," Thomas agreed. "It is likely home to squatters now. Come, we should leave. I doubt anyone can use this factory at night as Abigail said. Not when it is in this kind of disrepair. Most likely, the whispers are just that."

"Maybe..." Ruth hummed as she walked around the side of the building, scaring a stray cat. Ruth stepped back as the cat launched itself across the street before returning to her examination of the building. One window looked large enough to climb through, but was closed and undamaged.

"Ruth, we should go," Thomas repeated as he wandered closer to her.

Ruth nodded, but didn't step away, instead experimentally pushing at the window. After a sharp push, she found that it had been jammed closed, rather than locked. It gave way, showing a big enough gap to easily pass through.

"Ruth, this isn't a good idea."

"This is our only lead. If it doesn't pan out, then there will be no harm done. If I may remind you, I will be charged with treason if we do not succeed, and I have an inkling that execution will not agree with me."

Thomas relented at that, only giving a small groan as Ruth climbed through the window, tearing her dress a little. Normally, she was so particular about keeping her clothes in good condition, but this was not the time for such worries.

Thomas followed close behind her, but Ruth was already far ahead, inspecting the large factory machines for signs of recent use.

"Careful," he told her. "There could be squatters."

"Then we shall have someone to ask about the rumours of mechanical men."

"There could also be criminals," he muttered as he came to stand beside her. "What if they spread the rumours to keep people away? Or what if the thief is selling the mechanical men as hired henchmen for criminals?"

"Then I shall be deeply offended. Slavery is bad enough without the slaves being forced to perform illegal acts."

"You know that many of these people will not see it as slavery. Perhaps they're American."

"Then I shall be even more offended. Michel is a person, so it stands to reason that his siblings will be as well."

Any further argument from Thomas was cut off by the sound of a gunshot. Ruth knocked Thomas to the ground, quickly finding that the gunman had missed.

"I think someone doesn't want us here," Ruth muttered as she scrambled behind one of the machines.

There were several more clanging sounds of bullets hitting the machine shielding them.

"That is perhaps an understatement," Thomas replied, drawing a pistol of his own.

"Where did you get that?" Ruth demanded as he shot around the corner of the machine.

"You didn't honestly think I would agree to leave the ship without some kind of weapon, did you?"

"Well, yes. Where did you learn to fire a gun?"

"Now is hardly the time. Can you make it back to the window?"

"I think so."

"Then go. I shall cover you."

"But we're being shot at!"

"And we will continue to be shot at until we leave this building."

Ruth huffed, drawing up every ounce of her courage before bolting for the window. She heard footsteps behind her and assumed that they belonged to Thomas. The sound of gunshots refused to quiet as they ran, only stopping as they made their way around the corner.

Ruth looked back at the factory, just before it vanished from sight, and saw a pair of reflective eyes watching her leave from one of the upper windows.

"I think we have lost them," Thomas said, putting his gun away as he struggled for breath.

"The gunman was mechanical," Ruth told him. "I'm sure of it. But the machines haven't been functional for years. The factory isn't being used to make them."

"Then why post a lone gunman to protect it from intruders?"

"I don't know. The building was so decrepit, I can't imagine it having much use to anyone."

"Unless it was a trap for anyone who asked too many questions about the mechanical men."

"But how would they know that we would get the information?"

Thomas' gaze darkened as he stormed back the way they came.

5

It took Ruth a while to realise that Thomas was storming back to Abigail's. She had been so consumed with attempting to match his relentless pace that she didn't recognise the streets until they were right outside the café.

Thomas violently swung the door open before storming up to the counter.

"What ever is the matter?" Abigail asked as the patrons stared.

Ruth stood awkwardly, very aware that she and Thomas looked a complete state. Their clothing was covered in dust and torn in places. Ruth's hair had fallen from its clasp and they were both red in the face, clearly sweating from their run.

"The information you gave us led us straight into a trap," Thomas told her.

"A trap?"

"We were assaulted by a gunman in that factory and the machines had been out of use for years. There was nothing there, and hence no reason to send us there unless it was the meet our doom at the hands of that gunman."

"Thomas, I had no idea, you have to believe me."

"The thing is, Abigail, I don't know that I do. Your parents wrote you off, and you've been scraping by ever since. I don't know what you would trade away to get some scrap of the life you had before."

Abigail looked as if he had just slapped her.

"That was perhaps unnecessarily harsh," Ruth pointed out. "After all, we have no proof that she was the source of the trap." She turned to Abigail. "Where did you get your information? If someone is spreading false rumours, perhaps tracking them down will give us some more answers."

Abigail indicated to the back room, clearly very aware of her patrons' eyes on them. Ruth followed, though Thomas lingered for a moment before coming, clearly hesitant.

"One of Madam Aude's girls gave me the information," Abigail said in a low voice once the door had shut behind them. Thomas relaxed instantly, as if this information had explained part of Abigail's suspicious behaviour. "She comes in here sometimes, and she told me that one of Madam Aude's... *visitors* is rather loose with information regarding the mechanical men. When she told me of the rumours, she thought he was making it up. She hadn't heard of Ruth's Michel, so she just thought it was a fanciful tale to tell the girls."

"And he told her that the factory was used at night?"

"He told her of the rumours and strongly hinted that they were true. I suppose he was just exaggerating."

"Or someone else caught wind of his ramblings and decided to lay a trap for anyone inclined to investigate," Ruth speculated.

Thomas sighed. "Then I suppose we should go to Madam Aude's and find out who this man is. She owes me a favour."

"Good luck," Abigail said, very clearly aiming her words at Ruth alone.

Thomas looked sheepish at that. "Abigail, about what I said…"

"Thomas, I may have been cut off from certain luxuries, but I was also freed from their trappings. If you honestly think that I would take even the ghost of those shackles back, for any reason, then I suppose that you don't really know me all that well."

"I'm sorry."

"Save your apologies for someone who wants them and get out of my cafe."

6

"I should warn you. Madam Aude's establishment is… not a reputable one," Thomas said as they made their way back down the Parisian streets.

"What do you mean by that?"

"I mean that she provides a certain kind of… entertainment."

"Please, Thomas, speak plainly."

His face flushed bright red. "It's a brothel," he eventually muttered so low that Ruth had to strain to hear.

"A brothel?" she hissed back at him. "Thomas, honestly, how are you in acquaintance with the proprietor of such an establishment?"

His face started to turn positively crimson. "It can be incredibly difficult to meet certain needs when you have unique tastes," he defended, still keeping his voice at just a whisper.

Ruth shook her head, not believing her ears.

"It's fine for you. You don't have to deal with such needs."

"No, I just have to have the Queen's favour to keep from having to marry a man I built."

"Which is exactly why you have no room to judge."

Ruth sighed. "Well, no, I suppose not. But, Thomas, are we heading there now? What if we are seen entering such an establishment?"

"By who? This is Paris, my dear. There is a reason I came here for my excursions, rather than staying in England."

"I suppose that makes sense…"

Thomas' face gradually shifted back to its regular colour as they made their way to a different part of the city. Ruth's feet were starting to hurt from the walking, but she had yet to see a Fralsen in the streets. She wondered if they were exclusive to England.

"Do people always walk around the city?" Ruth asked.

"Fralsens were banned last year after an unfortunate accident. I had hoped that your rival technology would find success in markets that had rejected the Fralsens as too dangerous, but obviously that project became Michel."

"Yes, and I'm not even sure how he gained sentience, so I would be reluctant to try to create a non-sentient mechanical mind from the same plans."

"What about if you drew up completely different plans?"

"I'm not sure that I could sufficiently forget my original plans. And, even if I could, there would be no guarantee that a sentient mind would not eventually emerge, as happened with Michel."

"Then I suppose it was never meant to be. Never mind, you have more than enough other ideas."

"Not that they will be of any use if I'm executed."

Thomas gave her a sympathetic look. "They won't execute you. They wouldn't dare. The amount of potential progress the British Empire would lose if you were killed…"

"Which brings us the the rather unsettling question of what they might do to keep my mind working if I am executed…"

Thomas frowned. "What do you mean?"

"Well, ever since I created Michel, other inventors and scientists have been speculating what they might be able to do with the technology."

"Beyond creating more mechanical men?"

"Well, yes, given that the Queen outlawed creating more of them. One thought has been that, if it's possible to create a new mind, why could we not transfer one?"

"Transfer a mind?"

"Yes. From a human to a mechanical body."

"You could live forever."

"Think of what it would do to the line of succession."

"Queen Victoria could live forever as a mechanical woman."

"I honestly can't decide how I feel about that, which is why I have always been glad that the plans had never left my hands. At least, until now. It's not just a mechanical army, Thomas. This is the stepping stone to the next technological revolution."

Thomas sighed, shaking his head. "And now it's in the hands of a random thief. That is honestly terrifying."

"Quite. I certainly hope that we can find answers in this… *establishment* of yours."

"As I said, Madam Aude owes me a favour. If she knows anything, she will tell us."

"I suppose I would be happier not knowing how you came to be in a situation where she owes you a favour?"

He took a moment to think before saying, "Yes, you probably would be."

She sighed, shaking her head. "You're secretly some kind of scoundrel, aren't you?"

He smiled. "I had some fun in my youth."

Before Ruth could enquire into exactly what he meant by that, Thomas stopped outside a rather unassuming building.

"This is it," he told her. "You might want to prepare yourself. The last thing we need is for you to offend anyone before we get the information we need."

"Offend anyone?"

"Yes, with your delicate sensibilities. It would do a great deal to help if you would agree to reserve any judgement until we are back on the ship."

Ruth frowned, a little unsettled at what she might encounter if Thomas felt that such a warning was necessary.

As soon as Ruth stepped through the threshold, she was bombarded by a potent mix of opium and sweat that saturated the air.

"Remember what I said," Thomas said lowly to her as they walked through the dimly lit hallway, and Ruth realised that she had been frowning.

She focused on loosening her stiff expression and posture, but it was incredibly difficult when she could hear moaning through the walls that put her on edge.

Ruth had always been fairly agnostic on the idea of other people… being *intimate*. It had never been something she had wanted, and definitely not something worth giving up her independence to someone else for, so she had never really thought all that much about the particulars.

Now she was being faced with them and she had to admit that it caused her skin to crawl. The idea of so much *touching* had her clutching at her skirts, gripping the fabric so hard that her knuckles went white, the sensation grounding her as she focused on following Thomas.

A young, well-dressed man stood waiting for them at the end of the hall.

"Thomas," he greeted with a small smile. "I hadn't thought to see you around here again."

"I was in the city."

"And you have brought a companion with you," he noted, his eyes raking across Ruth in a way that made her feel naked despite her heavy layers. "Not to your taste, though. Tell me, ma chérie, are you here to learn of your own tastes?"

Ruth did her best not to balk. "I don't *have* tastes."

Thomas gave her a slightly disapproving look before turning back to the man. "Is Madam Aude available? I have business to discuss with her."

The man nodded, leading Thomas and Ruth through one of the doors and up a flight of stairs. He knocked on one of the doors three times.

"Come in," a voice called from the other side.

The man opened the door to reveal a room. It, like the rest of the establishment, was dimly lit, and was clearly for entertaining guests. Though, not for entertaining in the sense of the rest of the establishment, Ruth assumed, given the lack of bed. In all, it seemed thoroughly ordinary. As did the rotund woman wandering the room as she pinned up her curly black hair. Ruth had expected the women of the establishment to wear scandalously revealing clothing, but the woman's light green dress could have been taken from Ruth's wardrobe. Or, rather, a smaller version of it could have been.

"Thomas, my dear, it has been too long," the woman - Madam Aude, Ruth assumed - said as they entered. "And you have brought a friend."

The man who had led them in seemed to have concluded that he had finished his job, leaving the room and shutting the door behind him.

"This is my niece, Ruth. Ruth, this is Madam Aude," Thomas introduced.

"A pleasure, my dear," Madam Aude said as she indicated for the to take a seat. "Tea?"

"Please," Thomas replied as he and Ruth sat down on two of the chairs.

Madam Aude moved over to a teapot with an odd contraption around it. After she had filled the teapot with water from a jug, she flicked a switch on the contraption.

"So, what brings you here? I thought your trips to Paris were behind you." Madam Aude had almost no French accent, but she still pronounced Paris without the s.

"It's rather a long story," Thomas began with a tired sigh as the teapot began to produce steam, the water seemingly boiling within.

"Are we short on time?" Madam Aude asked.

"Aren't we always?"

Madam Aude smiled as she continued to make the tea. "You were always too quick-witted for your own good. A man like you should be settled down by now. You could have found a nice husband, but no. You're too busy being clever in London."

"Even Paris isn't far enough away to escape the scandal if I ran off with a man."

Madam Aude rolled her eyes. "You always cared too much for your reputation."

"Perhaps, but that is not why I'm here. We are here to catch a thief."

"And you came to my establishment? I know I cater to all kinds, but I do not do business with criminals."

Ruth frowned, taking a moment to remember that brothels were legal in France. Paris truly was like a different world, even if the streets weren't so different.

Madam Aude poured the tea that had finally finished brewing before bringing it to them.

"Thank you," Thomas said as he took his tea. "And you may not deal with criminals knowingly, but that doesn't mean that it's not possible."

Madam Aude sighed as she sat opposite them after passing Ruth her tea. "I suppose I must agree there."

"I have heard a rumour that one of your visitors comes accompanied by mechanical men."

"Now, Thomas, you know as well as anyone that I offer discretion. I can't go around giving away private details about my customers."

"Except he stole them!" Ruth interjected. "Or, rather, he stole the plans for them from me. No one was supposed to have that technology."

Madam Aude regarded her carefully. "Except for you, hmm?"

"I was never going to use it. Not again. Certainly not to build slaves."

"And it's your right to decide how people should or should not use this technology?"

"As the one who built it, yes. If they build mechanical armies or slaves, I will be complicit."

"And what if they built mechanical doctors? Men who could deal with plagues without the fear of becoming ill. What about dangerous work like mining? How many lives could be spared if you shared the technology?"

"How many jobs lost," Thomas countered. "Reintroducing slave labour would ruin the economy."

"And they would still be slaves," Ruth countered. "Unless you let them choose their path and paid them, but no one will enforce that. Regardless, that is beside the point."

"Is it? You want me to believe that you have been wronged to such a degree that I should violate my own code and risk my reputation to help you find justice. A thief may be on the wrong side of the law, but they may have had good reason for their theft."

"Can you help us or not?" Ruth asked, tired of the ethics lesson.

Madam Aude took on a contemplative look.

"You owe me a favour," Thomas reminded her.

"And you wish to use it over this?"

"Of course."

"Then so be it. He will be here tomorrow at six."

"Thank you."

7

Ruth was aware that she was being particularly quiet on the walk back to the airship. Ruth had never been one for idle chat, which meant that Thomas was used to having mostly one-sided conversations. Though, as he talked on their way back, his niece couldn't help but notice that he kept steering it in one particular direction.

"I was thinking about something Edgar was saying about how we should stop the production of these mechanical men once we find them."

"Edgar?" Ruth asked with a raised eyebrow.

"Captain Hall," he clarified with a slight blush.

"Ivy was right; you are infatuated with him."

"I am not!"

"First James, now Captain Hall. Is it the uniforms?"

He folded his arms. "Now, really, Ruth, I hardly think-"

"I am taking that as a yes."

He huffed a little. "Ivy is a terrible influence on you, you know."

"I thought I was the terrible influence on her. At least, that's what you said when you found her slumped over her desk after working through the night."

"You're both terrible for each other. I dread to think of the effect you both have on Michel. The poor boy is going to pick up some terrible habits."

"'Boy'? You speak as if he is a child."

Thomas frowned. "Ruth, in many ways, he is. He is still learning about the world. It does not seem unreasonable that he would need guidance, not unlike that of a parent. Guidance that you and Ivy have already set about providing."

"I suppose that is one way to look at the situation…" Ruth grumbled. "Though, I wonder, if Ivy and I were men, would you put such maternal connotations on the matter?"

"Possibly. Since I am not in that situation, I couldn't tell you. But that doesn't mean that I am wrong."

"No, it simply irritates me."

"I have never seen a woman run so far from the prospect of motherhood."

"I am perfectly agnostic on the prospect of motherhood. I simply don't think of Michel as a child. Naive, perhaps, but he has a fully developed brain, albeit a mechanical one. He learns new concepts quickly; he is just starting from scratch."

Anything else Thomas had to say was cut off by their arrival back at the airship.

"You're back!" Ivy exclaimed with a grin as Ruth and Thomas made their way back onto the bridge.

"Ivy was getting restless," Michel explained.

Ivy folded her arms as she made a face at the mechanical man. "Of course I was! It's boring up here, and Captain Hall wouldn't let me tinker with his equipment."

"You're not trained as one of our mechanics," Captain Hall said in a tired voice that told Ruth that he had probably been arguing the point with her for several hours. He turned to Ruth and Thomas. "So, did you learn anything new on your excursion?"

"I learned that Thomas has friends in odd places," Ruth commented, mostly to Ivy, who smirked in a way that suggested that she already knew that.

Thomas elbowed his niece slightly before turning back to Captain Hall. "We have learned of someone using mechanical men as guards. We know where he will be tomorrow at six. Our plan is to confront the man. Hopefully, we will be able to get some answers from him."

"If he's bringing guards, you should have protection as well," Captain Hall said.

"Too many people would draw attention to us."

"Then just you and one of my best men. Perhaps I will accompany you myself."

Ruth rolled her eyes. "In case you two are forgetting, you need me. Who knows what information about the mechanical men you may need."

Captain Hall sighed. "You cannot defend yourself."

"I'll figure something out. Some weakness of theirs that I can take advantage of. Not to mention, you and Thomas won't be of much use against them either. Guns stand very little chance of working."

"I would still rather not put a civilian woman in harm's way."

Michel stepped forward. "I could go with her and protect her. Ruth is the one most likely to find a way to stop them, and I would be fighting them on even ground. The two of us would be the best bet."

"You would only draw attention looking like that," Captain Hall protested.

Ruth folded her arms. "There is a reason we originally pretended Michel was French. The fashions are so outrageous here, no one will notice a man in a mask."

Captain Hall sighed. "I suppose you're committed to this, aren't you?"

"Of course. This is my mess and I am the best one to fix it."

"I'm not happy about this."

"You don't have to be. This is my mission. You're not in charge; you're just here to keep an eye on me."

He frowned at her, but couldn't dispute her point. His job was to make sure she didn't escape, nothing more.

"Come on," Ruth said to Ivy and Michel before leaving the room.

Michel didn't join Ruth and Ivy in the workshop. He decided to explore the ship on his own instead.

"His natural curiosity is fascinating," Ivy commented as she and Ruth entered the workshop. "Do you have any idea how that came about?"

"None at all. Michel's sentience is as much of a mystery to me as anyone. Which, I have to say, is quite infuriating. But there is little I can do to figure it out without poking around in his head, which I am loathed to do. Who knows what damage my own curiosity could cause?"

Ivy smiled as Ruth pulled out the designs she had been working on during the trip over.

"You really do care about him," Ivy said. "I imagine most inventors in your situation would be far more interested in replicating their work than helping it to develop as a person."

"Well, I don't know about that. This seems like the most basic of human kindness to me."

"And to think, some people talk about how those with an inventor's disposition are incapable of such things."

"Well, that is exactly why I have never held psychology in particularly high regard."

Ivy snorted at that. "Maybe they're prejudiced against you because you're more likely to offend them."

"Then they need to develop thicker skin, which is hardly my concern." Ruth lapsed back into silence as she circled a section of the chest of the mechanical man.

"The aether core?" Ivy asked with a raised eyebrow. "Do you think that could possibly be a weakness?"

"If we could disrupt it, they would power down completely."

"Almost like remotely activating a heart attack in a person?"

"Exactly."

"But how would you go about doing that?"

"That is the question, isn't it? But, given how well it seemed to work and how little we know of Michel's sentience, I have spent a great deal of time reading any research on aether I could find. I think I could use another aether core to create a pulse that, at the right frequency, could disrupt another core."

"Do we even have another aether core on board?"

"I brought a few along with my tools. Though I may not have disclosed that to Thomas or Captain Hall. You know how jumpy the untrained can be around aether."

"You really are prepared for any mechanical occasion, aren't you?"

"If nothing else."

"But, if you're going with Michel tomorrow, wouldn't the pulse shut him off as well?"

Ruth sighed. "I'm going to have to find a way to direct the energy into some sort of beam, rather than a blast."

"Do you think you can manage that before six tomorrow evening?"

"Hopefully. Though I may need your help. Firstly, do you think you could set about acquiring some coffee for us? I fear tea may not be strong enough."

8

Ruth was roused from her work some time later by a knock at the door.

"Could you finish soldering that together?" she asked Ivy, who readjusted her goggles before nodding.

Ruth headed to the door, opening it to see Captain Hall and Michel there.

"Are you ready to leave?" Captain Hall asked her. "You should have just enough time to change before heading out if you wish to arrive there for six."

"I believe I am, yes. Just..."

"Soldering is done!" Ivy called over her shoulder before removing her goggles and picking up the small contraption. It was a brass container, built around a cylindrical aether core. One end of the container had a handle and trigger, and the other was a directional rod.

"It's a gun?" Captain Hall asked.

"It's an aether disruptor," Ruth corrected sharply.

"It looks like a gun."

"It fires a burst that disrupts other aether sources. It will be effective against mechanical men and little else." She frowned at the weapon in Ivy's hands. "Or, rather, I don't know what effect it will have on humans. And I have no intention of finding out."

"But it will stop mechanical men?"

Ivy stepped towards the workbench at that, placing another aether core on the surface. It was giving off the same eerie blue glow as the one in the weapon.

"Watch this," she said to Captain Hall before pulling her goggles back down over her eyes. Ruth followed her lead as Ivy stepped back before aiming the aether disruptor at the core on the workbench.

"What's supposed to happen?" Captain Hall asked, just a second before Ivy fired the weapon.

The directional rod glowed with a loud whine, causing a sphere of light to bloom out around it. Then, so quickly that if one blinked they could have missed it, a straight, thin beam of white light burst forth, striking the core on the bench. The aether core's glow increased to a bright white light before sputtering out with a slightly distressing screech.

"Is that it?" Captain Hall asked, clearly having expected more damage than the dark aether core.

"That will be enough," Ruth assured him. "If the aether core is defunct, the mechanical man will be nothing more than a collection of metal shaped like a man."

Captain Hall raised a sceptical eyebrow. "And you're sure that it will work when the aether core is in the mechanical man's chest?"

"As sure as I can be without testing it, but seeing as there is no way to do that…"

Captain Hall gave Michel a pointed look.

Ruth felt fury flood her stomach and stretch out to her limbs, causing her to grip at her skirts tightly. "As I said, there is no way to test it."

Captain Hall returned her glare. "You had better get ready if you want to keep your appointment."

He turned and stalked off, leaving Ruth to glare at his back.

"The captain doesn't seem too fond of me," Michel noted.

Ruth sighed, giving him a weary smile. "Nor me. Had we been born a few hundred years earlier, I fear he may have tried to burn me as a witch or some such nonsense."

Ivy gave a disagreeing hum. "Maybe it's not so much your intellect he doesn't like, but the possibility that you might be a traitor."

"But I'm not."

"Yes, but he doesn't know that. And if he does start to like any of us, and then we betray him, he will feel worse for it."

"Well then, let's get these plans back and prove him wrong. Not least because Thomas' infatuation is going to quickly get tiresome."

After a quick change of clothes, Ruth and Michel made their way back to the brothel, with Ruth carefully focusing on remembering the route she and Thomas had taken the day before.

"Where exactly are we heading and what should we expect?" Michel asked her after a few minutes of turning his head incessantly to get a good look at all of the oddities of the streets. It was perfectly understandable, Ruth thought, given that he had barely been outside in London. Wandering through the streets always seemed too risky. At first, any extra eyes on Michel increased the chances of him being identified as mechanical. After everyone knew about Michel, Ruth doubted they would be able to walk freely in the streets without drawing unwanted attention. Michel had never protested that, so Ruth had always assumed that he preferred to stay inside over being ambushed by crowds of people who wanted to gawk at him. Now, as she watched his fascination at his environment, she wondered if she had been wrong.

"A brothel," she said, deciding to answer his question and stow her own away for later.

"Brothel?"

"An establishment where people pay for sex."

"Ah. Yes, Ivy found me an anatomy book and explained the process."

Ruth had to hold in a laugh at that. "Well, I doubt that knowledge will be needed. Madam Aude will take us to the room he usually books, and when he arrives, we will corner him and ask where he got his mechanical guards."

"But those mechanical guards will be with him."

"Well, yes. Hopefully between my disrupter, and your comparable abilities, we should be able to stop them."

"Hopefully," he agreed as they arrived.

Instead of the man from the day before, Madam Aude was waiting to greet them.

"Where is Thomas?" she asked.

"I thought I would bring Michel instead. He will probably be more useful if things go poorly."

Madam Aude responded with a glare. "I sincerely hope you will do everything in your power to make sure things *don't* go poorly. I am extending you an enormous courtesy, after all. The least you could do is try to keep my place of business intact."

"We shall do our best," she assured the older woman.

Madam Aude gave a look that suggested that she didn't quite trust Ruth to follow through on that promise, but she led them upstairs regardless.

The room she led them to looked far more like what Ruth would have expected than the room she had met Madam Aude in the day before. There was a large bed covered in plush pillows taking up most of the room, but there were also wooden structures that Ruth presumed must be some kind of chair, but she had no idea how it would work, or why anyone would choose to sit on something so bizarrely constructed.

"Francis will bring him up when he arrives," Madam Aude told them before leaving, closing the door behind her.

"Well, I suppose we now just have to wait," Ruth said before inspecting the disrupter. She wanted to be sure that it was in working condition, and she desperately needed the distraction.

"Ruth," Michel said, stepping forward in that way that she knew meant that he was trying to gauge just how wrapped up in her work she was.

"Yes?"

"I wanted to thank you."

"For what?"

"For standing up for me when Captain Hall insinuated that you should…" He trailed off, leaving Ruth with the sense that he was disquieted at the thought of his potential demise. Of course, it was natural that he would be, but Ruth was never sure which common human behaviours and attitudes Michel would or wouldn't have.

"Of course I did. I wasn't going to kill you just to test this gun."

"I just… I don't know what I would do without you looking out for me."

"You would be fine," Ruth assured him. "If you ever wanted to strike out on your own, I mean."

He frowned. "Is that something I should want?"

"I don't know. I just mean, if you ever tire of tagging along with me, don't feel that you have to stay."

"I will remember that, but I cannot envisage a future where I would want to leave you and Ivy."

Ruth couldn't help but smile at that assurance, but before she could respond, there was a knock at the door. It opened a moment after and one of Madam Aude's men ushered a portly older gentleman into the room, quickly shutting the door behind him.

The man frowned before saying something in French.

"I should have possibly seen that coming," Ruth said. All of Thomas' contacts speaking English had made her forget that they were, in fact, in another country.

"He's asking where the usual girl is," Michel said.

Ruth pulled out the disrupter and aimed it at the man, who immediately took a step back, his eyes wide as he started sweating profusely. "Tell him that I'll shoot if he calls for his guards."

Michel relayed Ruth's command in French before turning back to her. "I thought you said that the disrupter wouldn't work against humans."

"He doesn't know that," Ruth figured, trying to get some kind of read on the man in front of her, other than 'terrified'. "At least, he doesn't, assuming he truly knows no English."

"I didn't think of that," Michel admitted apologetically.

"No matter. Ask him how he came across those mechanical guards of his."

Michel repeated her words back in French. The man shook his head frantically as he replied.

"A friend of his operated as the middleman. He swears that he doesn't know the manufacturers, and he has never met them."

"Ask who his friend is. Their name will be better than nothing."

"And if he warns his friend before we can find them?"

Ruth sighed. "I don't know. But it's still the best lead we have."

Before Michel could ask, there was a knock at the door, quickly followed by someone who sounded eerily like Michel shouting through in French.

"Tell him to tell them he's fine," Ruth hissed as the terrified man looked to her, clearly afraid that she could be spooked and shoot him.

Before Michel could relay the command, the guards clearly decided that something was wrong, kicking down the door.

Ruth responded instantly by firing her disrupter at the first guard. He immediately keeled over, as she had caught him in mid-step. The second guard seemed barely disturbed by his brother going down, heading straight for Ruth.

Michel jumped between them, slamming the second guard against the wall as his charge made a scrabbling escape out of the room on all fours.

"Shoot him!" Michel yelled at her as the guard tried to push him off.

"I can't without risking hitting you."

"Then get ready."

Ruth nodded as she levelled her disrupter.

Michel launched himself away from the guard and Ruth pulled the trigger.

The disrupter spluttered in her hand.

The guard used the chance to get across the room, launching itself out of the covered window, causing daylight to flood the bedchamber, momentarily blinding Ruth.

"Are you okay?" she heard Michel ask her.

"Yes, I'm fine, can you go after the guard?"

"No, he's too far for me to catch up, but I think I have a better idea."

As Ruth regained her sight, she saw Michel head out into the corridor and pick up the man who was still struggling to get away, dragging him back to the room.

Michel said something to him in French.

Ruth raised an eyebrow as the man answered, waiting for Michel to translate.

"I asked him where the guard went, given that the mission was to protect him."

"What did he say?"

"They're meant to return to the manufacturer if they're damaged."

"Even if it means abandoning their mission?"

Michel relayed the question.

"Only if they fear that they may become inoperable," Michel translated back from the man. "It seems that our thief doesn't want anyone else to get their hands on the mechanical men."

"Possibly because there is a way to track them using the parts."

"Or because they don't want anyone else to be able to reverse-engineer the designs. Right now, you're the only other party with the knowledge, and you are refusing to sell them. That gives them a monopoly."

Ruth sighed. "Well, we have one of their defunct guards now. Hopefully I will be able to use the parts or something to identify where he came from, and where his brother went." She turned to look at the terrified man. "Tell him that he can go as long as he promises not to tell anyone about us."

Michel relayed the message back to the man, who nodded enthusiastically. As soon as Michel and Ruth stepped away from him, he bolted, leaving them alone.

Ruth moved over to inspect the downed guard as another thought came to her. "Of course, he wouldn't have been able to tell them much more than the other guard probably will. We may have lost our element of surprise."

9

Ruth got to work as soon as she arrived back at the ship, and didn't stop until the next morning. Ivy and Michel stayed by her side, helping to dissect the mechanical guard.

Ivy was more than happy to dive into the work, but Michel seemed noticeably disturbed. Ruth made an effort to finish her work as quickly as possible.

"What is it?" Michel asked as Ruth hesitated over the now defunct aether core.

"Do you see this?" she asked as she inspected the valves around the core with a pair of tweezers. "The aether transfer process they're using is based on my old designs. It creates a harmonic resonance as the aether is transferred into kinetic energy. I eliminated it because it can interfere with navigational equipment, but if I alter the valves around your aether core, I can have them resonate in tandem. You should be able to use that resonance to figure out where in the city they're concentrated."

"Which will mean their factory," Ivy continued with a grin.

"Hopefully."

Ruth was back on the ground almost immediately with Michel and Ivy in tow. Modifying Michel to detect other mechanical men had been far easier than she had thought it might be, which she was glad for. After Michel's obvious discomfort at his non-operational counterpart, Ruth figured that a walk through Paris would be the best thing for him.

"Can you feel anything?" Ruth asked him, wondering if her tracking system was working.

"Yes, I think so. Like a light buzzing coming from all directions."

Ruth frowned.

"There are probably mechanical men all over the city," Ivy reasoned. "Not many, but enough to give signals in every direction."

Ruth nodded in agreement before turning back to Michel. "Is it stronger in any particular direction?"

Michel pivoted on his heel, making several rotations before abandoning that attempt in favour of walking in a small circle. The circle eventually became a spiral as Michel kept walking, and Ruth became hyper aware of how many eyes were now on them.

Michel eventually came to a dead stop.

"That way," he said, pointing down the street.

"Lead the way," Ruth told him with a grin.

Ivy and Ruth followed close behind Michel as he led them down the Parisian streets. His pace was swift, thanks to some of the more recent additions Ruth had made to his legs, and Ruth found herself wishing that she had worn fewer skirts. She was, after all, in Paris. Anything went here, and it probably wouldn't get back to London, if Thomas' escapades were anything to go by.

Eventually, Michel slowed with a frown. "I think we are almost there. It is almost unpleasant now."

"I'm sorry," Ruth said. "I will deactivate it as soon as we've found them."

Michel nodded before leading them to the row of factories. Ruth recognised that they couldn't be more than a couple of streets away from the abandoned factory she and Thomas had encountered the mechanical gunman in.

Michel approached one of the factories, and Ruth could hear the sound of metal straining through the wall. The machines inside were being pushed to their limits.

Michel walked around the building in a full circle before declaring, "This is it. There are... so many inside."

"Dozens?" Ruth asked, a little disquieted at the thought. That many would be a force to be reckoned with.

Michel shook his head, his reflective eyes seeming wider. Ruth briefly wondered if he was afraid.

"At least a hundred of my siblings are inside," he eventually managed, chilling her to the bone.

"We'll do everything we can to free them," Ruth said, knowing that she was making an assumption that they didn't want to be there. Still, saying, "And I can deactivate them if they have chosen the wrong side," seemed a little callous. Especially when Michel had just referred to them as his siblings.

"Look," Ivy said beneath her breath.

Ruth turned to her to see that she was looking up at a balcony across the street. Ruth just barely saw a pair of reflective eyes watching them before their owner disappeared.

"Come on," Ruth said. "We should get back."

10

"That had better not be what I think it is," Ruth said as Captain Hall placed an aether powered device in front of them.

"What is it?" Ivy asked.

"It's a bomb," Captain Hall answered as he glared at Ruth, daring her to go through with her clear protest.

"We're not blowing up a factory. There's no way to ensure no collateral."

"The damage to the surrounding area would be minimal."

"But still existent. And we have no idea how guilty anyone is. The workers may not know what they're involved in."

Captain Hall sighed. "If you have another plan, I would be happy to hear it, but we cannot leave until we are sure that no more mechanical men can be produced."

Ruth fell silent, finding her lack of military strategy knowledge a hindrance.

"Maybe we can evacuate the factory or something," Ivy suggested.

"Do what you will," Captain Hall told them. "Just don't jeopardise the mission."

In the end, Ruth decided that she and Michel should be the only ones to go. She knew how to set the bomb, and she was also the one most familiar with her plans, meaning that she could get them back without the fear that she had picked up the wrong pieces of paper.

If anyone else accompanied her, it would have drawn more attention, but Michel, while built to slightly different specifications, would hopefully blend in with the other mechanical men.

"Ruth," Michel said as they finally approached the factory. "I am… uneasy."

"That is to be expected. I would be lying if I said that I was at ease with this myself."

"I know, but… I am worried that I will prove insufficient."

"Insufficient?"

"When it comes to protecting you. If there are as many of my siblings inside as we suspect… I could stand a chance against that many humans, but not mechanical men."

Ruth stepped forward, trying to give him a reassuring smile. "That is why the plan is stealth. With any luck, we won't have to fight anyone."

Michel nodded, but didn't seem entirely convinced. Ruth thought it was sweet that he was so concerned for her, but this wasn't the time.

"Follow me," she said as she found a side door that hadn't been locked.

The factory floor was so busy that Ruth felt immediately secure in the assumption that no one would notice her. She had dressed herself in a plain brown dress and tucked her hair into a plain braid to avoid drawing attention.

Everyone on the floor was noticeably scruffy, but Ruth spotted a particularly well dressed man climbing the stairs up the opposite wall.

"I suspect the offices may be upstairs," Ruth said, indicating to the small room that the man had entered. It was suspended from the wall by metal beams and seemed to make up the entirety of the upper floor. "If the plans are anywhere, they will be there."

"Perhaps, but now we know that it is occupied," Michel said.

Just as Ruth was about to curse their luck, the man headed back down, holding something she couldn't see in his hands.

"Now it might not be," Ruth ventured, leading Michel around by the wall to the stairs, doing her best to avoid the eye-line of the well-dressed man until he left the factory.

"What if it is?" he asked.

Ruth shrugged as she led him up the stairs. "Say we got lost. If all else fails, I shall cry."

"Cry?"

"Men never know what to do with a crying woman."

They reached the top of the stairs and Ruth could see through the office window that it was empty.

"Keep guard while I look for the plans," she said to Michel as she brought one of her tools from her pinafore and used it to unlock the office door.

Michel nodded, standing in the door as she crept through.

The office was a mess, with pieces of paper everywhere. It looked like someone had been trying to add to her designs, but she could tell at a glance that most of the additions would only ruin the mechanical men.

She rifled through the papers, sure that the original designs had to be there somewhere. After a few moments, however, someone spoke from outside the door, forcing her to duck down behind the desk.

"What are you doing up here? Mechs aren't authorised to be in the office."

"I'm not in the office," Michel replied as Ruth dared to peek over the desk, seeing that he was being questioned by the well-dressed man, who was now followed by two mechanical men of his own.

"You know what I mean," the man replied with an irritated wave of his hand. "What are you doing up here?"

"I'm not sure," Michel said after a moment.

The man sighed. "Great, just what I need: malfunctioning mechs."

"I'm not sure," Michel repeated, seemingly playing up the malfunctioning angle.

"Get him down to maintenance," the man told the two mechanical men - or mechs, as he appeared to be calling them - behind him.

"Incorrect model," one of the mechs replied.

"What?"

"Incorrect model."

"What do you mean 'incorrect model'? Just get him down to maintenance."

"Incorrect model."

The man looked as if he was about to hit the mech, but he paused as realisation seemed to strike him. He turned back to Michel. "The mech's right. You don't look like them. Your face is wrong. You're one of The Owl's machines, aren't you?"

"I'm not sure," Michel repeated, impressing Ruth with his commitment to the role.

The man smiled. "Well, you're definitely not one of mine. She sent you, didn't she? You're a spy to retrieve her plans." His smile faltered. "Which means that she knows that we're here." He shook his head. "It's not as if she can storm the factory with British soldiers. Not on French soil. I'm guessing that's why she sent you."

"I'm not sure."

The man rolled his eyes. "Take him away," he told the other mechs.

Ruth clutched at her disrupter, but didn't otherwise move. She hadn't been able to shorten the refractory period, meaning that she could only take out one of the mechs. Not to mention that it wouldn't help against the man.

If she revealed herself, there was no doubt that she too would be captured, which would do Michel no good.

Ruth felt the weight of the bomb - split into parts so that it wouldn't go off - beneath her skirts. She knew that if Captain Hall had been there, he would have told her to ignore Michel and complete the mission.

But he wasn't there, and Ruth wasn't about to abandon Michel.

She gave the office another quick look, finding a locked safe, before sneaking back out.

11

"Let me get this straight," Captain Hall said with a murderous glare after Ruth had finished informing him of how the mission had gone, "you not only failed to get the plans back and to set off the bomb, you also got your much more advanced mechanical man kidnapped by those who could reverse-engineer his systems?"

Ruth nodded solemnly, but Ivy stepped forward.

"You need to back off right now. She did everything she could and yelling at her isn't going to change anything. Our focus right now should be helping Michel, not squabbling like toddlers."

Captain Hall had the decency to look just the tiniest bit shaken at Ivy's words. "Our priority is still the deactivation of the factory."

"I don't think anyone believes that has changed," Ivy agreed. "But we also need to recover Mech. If for no other reason than to stop others from reverse engineering him. Ruth got a good look at the facility while she was there. We should be able to formulate a better plan now."

"Assuming they haven't changed their security."

"By tomorrow? Possible, but I doubt by much."

Thomas stepped forward at that. "They can do this, Edgar. Please, trust that."

Captain Hall turned his glare to Thomas, but it softened immediately. "Alright. But at sunset tomorrow, I am going in with my men and we are ending this once and for all."

"They can work with that," Thomas assured him before turning to Ruth and Ivy. "Can't you?"

They nodded in unison.

The new plan was sorted by the early hours of the morning, and had Ruth and Ivy leaving the ship before sunrise, dressed in brown jumpsuits that greatly resembled those worn by the factory staff.

"Are you sure your spider can handle this?" Ivy asked, giving it a wary glance as it sneaked up Ruth's arm and under her sleeve.

Ruth shrugged. "I've not had time to work on it since we left London, but I can hope."

Ivy nodded, though it was clear that she didn't share her mentor's faith. "So, do you think there will be guards?"

"I guess we'll find out," Ruth said as they approached the streets surrounding the factory. "Can you see anything?"

"Let's see." Ivy pulled on a pair of goggles.

"What are those for?" Ruth asked, admiring the craftsmanship.

"Well, when my navigational system went up in flames, I decided a change of project was needed."

"Prudent."

"Quite. Well, when you were working on the tracking system for the mechanical men, I got an idea. I designed these goggles to pick up the traces of aether that are invisible to the naked eye. They'll be useless once it's more widely used, but for now they are letting me see how many mechanical men are here."

"Impressive. So, how many are there?"

"Several on the factory floor, but they keep walking in front of each other, so I can't get an accurate count. There are six in position in the surrounding buildings, presumably watching for us, and one on the upper floor of the factory. I would assume that last one is Michel."

"Alright," Ruth said. "Can you figure out how to get us around to the south side of the factory? There was another side entrance there, and I don't want to use the one from yesterday."

"Yes," Ivy said after a moment. "Back around that street and through the back alley. Follow me."

Ruth followed closely after Ivy, who kept looking up through the buildings they walked past, presumably checking their position in relation to the mechs and ensuring that they didn't move.

After several minutes of wandering, they arrived at the entrance.

"You're sure they didn't see us?" Ruth asked.

"As sure as I can be," Ivy said with a shrug as she pushed her goggles back up onto her hair.

"Then that'll have to do."

12

The factory floor was just as crowded as it had been the day before, which meant that it was just as noisy and steam still concealed a large part of the floor.

They would be expecting any intruders to head upstairs immediately, meaning that the floor wouldn't be so closely guarded.

"Can you ensure that the spider does its job?" Ruth asked as she let the mechanical creature climb down to her open palm, waiting for Ivy to receive it.

Ivy grimaced but nodded. "You owe me for this."

Ruth rolled her eyes. "You know, it's not a real spider."

"It's close enough."

Ruth stayed close to Ivy as the younger woman inspected the machines around her, looking for a weak spot. Ruth didn't interfere, for risk of setting Ivy on a path that she couldn't complete on her own, but she couldn't head to Michel until Ivy had completed her part of the plan.

Thankfully, Ivy didn't take too long in finding a machine that she could work with, whispering instructions to the spider before setting it off.

Ruth took that as her cue, heading for the stairs just as there was an almighty clash followed by a hissing noise. The guards near the stairs, along with all of the others, headed to the sabotaged machine. By the time they found her spider, she, Ivy and Michel would be hopefully long gone.

Ruth bounded up the stairs, taking them two at a time. She couldn't waste time when someone might be dissecting her friend.

She frowned. Was it still dissecting when they were mechanical?

She pushed away the morbid thought as she reached the office, thankfully finding it unlocked. She entered to see Michel alone, and shackled to the far wall.

"Michel!" she cried, hurrying over to him.

"Ruth, no!" he said as the door clicked closed behind her, quickly followed by a faint hissing noise. "It's a trap. Run!"

"I'm not leaving you," she said, her voice firm despite her thundering heart, but found herself choking back a cough as the room flooded with a white mist. "What is thiiiiiiissss..."

She was unconscious before she hit the floor.

13

Ruth awoke in a dark room that smelled faintly damp. She could feel that she was strapped to a chair with some rather thick rope, and the air around her had a deathly chill. Her hair and clothes felt slightly damp, though she couldn't figure out why. Her best guess was that whatever had knocked her out had caused her to sweat profusely as it passed through her system. It occurred to her that, if she was left alone for too long, she would probably dehydrate.

Though, she supposed that would happen anyway. It just might have taken longer before.

She wasn't sure how long she had spent trying to wriggle her way out of the ropes and hop on the chair so that it would break before a door opened at the other end of the room, finally allowing light through. All Ruth knew was that her wrists were raw and bleeding from her efforts, making her hands slick with blood.

The man from the day before entered the room, carrying a lamp in one hand, and a pistol in the other.

"So," he said as he put the lamp down on the floor next to him, just out of Ruth's reach, "you're The Owl. I can't say that I'm impressed."

"And you're the thief who stole my plans," Ruth replied, impressed by her own ability to keep her voice from wavering. "I was expecting someone... Well, not you."

His right eyebrow quirked up slightly. "Oh, I wasn't the one who stole from you. No, such messy work was someone else's job. I am simply the man who saw an opportunity that you were foolish enough to squander."

"Selling slaves? Even Americans don't do that anymore."

"They're not people," he countered. "It's not the same."

Ruth rolled her eyes. "Of course you would say that. Morality is easily bent by men like you when it becomes inconvenient."

"Men like me?"

Ruth just glared. "Men who are incapable of thinking of the consequences of their actions. Or, perhaps, you're incapable of caring."

"Says the woman fuelling the British Empire."

"I don't build weapons."

"Which, of course, absolves you of any wrongdoing the rest of your inventions may be put to. And what of your inevitable demise? What is to stop Queen Victoria from using your mechanical men in her army then? All I'm doing is preemptively evening the playing field."

"All for a tidy profit, I assume."

The man just grinned. "Well, that doesn't hurt. And I suppose you build your machines for free?"

Ruth couldn't come up with an answer to that fast enough.

The man in front of her lifted his pistol, bringing it right between her eyes.

Ruth couldn't help but shudder at that, though she did manage to withhold a whimper.

"I have a simple proposition for you," the man said. "Work for me instead, here in Paris. You can have all of the comfort of home, and all of the tools you could possibly need."

"And be considered a traitor to the Crown? You might as well pull that trigger now. I would be a dead woman."

"I have the means to keep you safe."

"Ah yes, your mechanical men? Well, unfortunately, I have managed to fashion a weapon to use against them, and the men who brought me here are aware of it. It won't take them long to build their own."

"Then you can improve the mechs so that this weapon no longer poses a problem."

"You are overestimating my abilities."

"Oh, I'm pretty sure that I'm not. So, what do you say? Work with me and live, or die here?"

Ruth sighed, not really seeing another way out.

"Fine. I suppose working with you can't be worse than death," she relented.

The man's grin widened as he put the pistol into a holster on his side and taking a knife out to replace it. He cut away the rope, and Ruth did her best not to flinch at his proximity.

"You've managed to create quite a mess of yourself," he said as he examined the damage to her wrists. "Not to worry, I have a doctor on staff. She can take a look once you're securely in the workshop."

Ruth nodded as he led her out of the dark room and to a dimly lit corridor. There were no windows or other doors, just a flight of stairs leading up. She assumed this meant that they were underground.

"In front of me," the man said, bringing his gun back out and holding it to the small of her back. "Any attempt to escape before we reach the workshop will result in your swift demise."

"Not if you shoot me there it won't," she muttered. She would still die if he didn't get her medical attention, but it wouldn't be swift.

He ignored her, instead pushing her up towards the light at the top of the stairs.

14

As Ruth reached the top of the stairs, she found that she was back on the factory floor. She must have been underneath the factory the whole time, she figured, as the man pushed her along the wall.

Ruth kept her eyes on the machinery, looking for a familiar glint of her own creation. She, of course, had no idea how long she had been unconscious. Perhaps Ivy had already left. Perhaps they only had moments before Captain Hall brought his men.

"You know that the people who brought me here know about this factory, right?" Ruth asked, her eyes still scanning.

"Of course. We are in the process of moving to another factory, but it will take time."

"They may not give you time. Especially if I don't report in."

"They won't risk hurting you."

"If that was true, they wouldn't have let me come here in the first place."

"Perhaps they had no choice. Perhaps you were the best bet for getting past the machines. Perhaps you didn't want to share your new weapon, for fear of it being used against your own mech."

Ruth just shrugged as she finally spotted the familiar glint of spider-like legs on top of one of the factory machines. She moved her hand so that three fingers were clearly visible against her leg, hoping that the predesignated parameters would kick in. She hadn't tested the visual input systems as thoroughly as the audio.

The spider scuttled away, and she hoped that was good for her.

The man brought her back upstairs to the office, but it no longer looked much like an office. Michel was still there, shackled to the wall, but the desk had been replaced with a workbench and everything else had been stripped out to provide more tools. She wondered just how quickly they had managed to change the room, and couldn't help but think that it was indicative of her being unconscious for longer than was preferable.

She wished that she had a window so that she could tell how close to sunset they were.

"Unshackle him," Ruth said to the man, indicating to Michel.

"Why?"

"Because he can help me and because it's inhumane."

He looked uncertain and Ruth sighed.

"Look, either you unshackle him, or I waste both of our time by doing it myself with the tools in here. Your choice."

The man took a moment to regard her carefully before reaching into his pocket to retrieve a key. He walked over to Michel and unshackled him before heading back to the door.

"Start working on a defence for your weapon," the man said as he paused at the door. "I'm going to start evacuating everyone with the vital equipment. I'll be back for you before sunset."

"With more knock-out gas?"

"We'll see."

He locked the door behind him.

Ruth sighed, turning back to Michel. "Oh, thank goodness you're alive," she said as she threw her arms around him. "Or, well, operational. I thought they might have tried to dismantle you."

"That was their plan, but then they decided to wait and see if you came for me. They didn't want to break me if they could get you to help them instead."

Ruth folded her arms. "Well, they have me now."

"I thought you wouldn't work with them. I was sure that they would end up killing you."

"I wasn't going to force their hand. Not when I still have a plan."

"Captain Hall's men storming the factory?"

"No. That's the final plan."

They heard a loud clash of metal below them and the floor shook.

"That's the current plan."

"What was that?" Michel asked.

"Ivy, I think. Can you help me get this door open?"

"If I could, he wouldn't have unshackled me."

"Hmm, you have a point there," Ruth agreed as she reached into her jumpsuit, extracting a smaller version of her disrupter from beneath her corset. "I'm very glad he didn't think to search me that thoroughly…"

"You built another disrupter?"

"Well, I couldn't easily conceal the bigger one. Not without rearranging my organs. This one was painful enough as it was…"

"And you used the same smaller aether core as for your spiders?"

"Exactly."

"Will it be able to disrupt the larger cores?"

"That is the question of the day, I'm afraid. Hopefully, it will at least give them pause, if nothing else."

"Well now, I'm just brimming with confidence."

Ruth smirked proudly at the appropriate use of sarcasm. "Well, the plan is not to need it at all." She moved over to the work bench, seeing the plans. "Is there any hope that these are the originals?"

Michel shook his head. "The man from before keeps them on him."

"Then we need to find him," Ruth said before rolling up the copies and placing them on the workbench, using the blowlamp to burn them to ash.

The door clicked open before they had the chance to figure out just how to do that. Ruth raised her disrupter, ready to stop any mechs that might try to move her, only to see her little spider move around the door from the lock.

"Aw, did Ivy send you back up to find us?" Ruth asked as she held her hand out, allowing the spider to step onto it.

It gave a little nod along with an affirmative click.

"Thank you. Do you think you can find the man in charge and attach yourself to him?"

It gave another nod before scuttling off.

"What good will that do?" Michel asked.

"Hopefully, Ivy's goggles will help us to track him down. We just need to find her."

"Her goggles?"

"Long story," Ruth said, heading out of the office door and down the stairs, running right into Ivy.

"Oh good," Ivy said with a relieved smile. "I was worried your spider might not have gotten you out."

"How long have we got until the machines break down?"

Ivy bit her lip before answering. "Weeeellll, I wouldn't exactly call it breaking down."

"What would you call it?"

"An explosive dismantling."

Ruth sighed. "We have to run, don't we?"

"That would be best."

Ruth followed close behind Ivy as they headed to the door, Michel keeping close behind her in turn. They bolted towards the closed door, all three of them staying as tight as they could in an effort not to lose each other in the chaos surrounding them. Once they made it, Ruth and Ivy moved to either side, allowing Michel to step up to the door. He brought his solid metal leg to the door and gave it a deafening kick, blowing it from its hinges.

They spilled out into the street, making it to the other side just as they heard a series of crashing noises that had Ruth clutch at her trouser leg so hard that the fabric began to rip apart at the seam down her thigh.

Ruth turned back to see that there was smoke billowing out through the door they had just escaped through, dissipating about halfway down to them.

"Did everyone else get out?" Ruth asked.

Ivy shrugged. "I think so. I didn't see anyone during our escape."

"What about the surrounding buildings? Will the fire spread?"

"The smoke isn't from an open flame, just the inside of the equipment. The machines will be beyond repair, but there shouldn't be any other damage."

Ruth gave a grateful nod at that before Michel spoke up.

"What about the man in charge?" he asked. "He is getting away with your plans."

Ruth turned back to Ivy. "My spider should be on him. Can you use your goggles to track it?"

She shrugged, bringing them back down over her eyes. She gave a frustrated hum, pulling them off to clean the smoke residue from them before putting them back on.

"I can't see it," she said as she looked around. "It's probably too small."

"Now what?" Michel asked.

Ruth bit her lip as her stomach churned. While destroying the factory was a move in the right direction, they still couldn't leave until they had the plans, and now that he knew that they were after him, the man would probably try to flee the city.

"Can't you use Michel to track them?" Ivy asked. "I mean, it worked with the other mechs."

"Yes, but that only worked because they were using the same aether cores. The spider has the smaller one." She waved her small disrupter in illustration.

"Can't you use your disrupter to track it?"

"I have no way of interpreting the resonance," Ruth said, before being struck by inspiration. "Actually, that might not be true. Come on, I need somewhere to work."

Abigail wasn't exactly happy with the three scruffy and dishevelled people taking up a table at her cafe, especially with one of them looking so obviously inhuman, but Ivy took the time to smooth things over as Ruth got to work.

"What did you say to calm her down?" Ruth asked as Ivy brought her a cup of coffee.

"I told her Thomas would more than pay for our visit here."

Ruth smirked. "I suppose that's one way to handle a social situation, but you can explain that to Thomas."

"Oh, I think that once we're no longer actually causing problems for Captain Hall, he will be more than distracted."

"And if not?"

"Then I will make sure to nudge the two of them together. It would be a shame if they let this whole thing get in the way of their happiness."

"You mean it would be a shame if an officer of the Crown let the fact that the man he is interested in is a possible traitor get in the way of their potential relationship?"

"Well, exactly."

Ruth shook her head as she continued to rearrange the metal parts around the disrupter. After a few moments, she finished with that section of her work, sitting back with a sigh as she started on her coffee.

"Is there anything I can help with?" Ivy asked.

Ruth was about to say no, as it was really a one-person job, but then she remembered that she was supposed to be teaching Ivy. Not that the girl had much left to learn, but Ruth felt bad that she probably hadn't been that attentive to her student. Ruth tended to leave the younger woman to her own projects, only giving her a helping hand when asked. It was an arrangement that suited Ruth quite well, but it hadn't occurred to her that Ivy might have expected more from her tutelage under the great Owl.

"I was going to hook this up as a secondary core for Michel," Ruth said, showing Ivy the small disruptor's rearrangement. It no longer had a handle or a trigger, just the barest of casing around the core. "It shouldn't take much reworking in his chest to attach it, and then he can use it to track down the spider."

"Okay," Ivy said, waiting expectantly.

Ruth realised she hadn't made her intent clear. "You should do it," she said. "Rather than just watching me, I mean."

"I..." She turned to Michel. "What if I break you?"

Michel gave one of his little half smiles. "I do not believe that you will. I trust you, Ivy."

Ruth got the distinct impression, by the way the younger woman quickly nodded silently, that Ivy would be blushing if her skin was lighter.

"I'll do my best," she promised, before turning back to Ruth.

Ruth nodded to show that she was still there and keeping an eye out, though she was sitting back in her chair and languidly sipping her coffee. She didn't want Ivy to think that she was perching like a hawk, just waiting for the smallest slip. Much like Michel, she trusted Ivy. The girl might have only just to get the hang of working on her own projects, but that was a far step up from simple maintenance and upgrading. Especially when she was already so familiar with Michel's make-up.

By the time Ruth was finished with her coffee, Ivy was pulling away from Michel's chest and lifting up her goggles.

"That should do it," she said, looking awkwardly between the other two.

"Well, time to see if it works," Ruth said as she sat up straight.

"It will," Michel said, and Ruth realised that she might have sounded as if she didn't believe in Ivy's abilities, which wasn't the case at all.

"Well then, try it," Ruth said.

Michel nodded, closing his eyes in concentration as he appeared to be trying to feel out the resonance of the new core.

"There," he said. "I can feel it, but it's much quieter than the other one. It may be difficult to find him with it this sensitive."

"Well, it's better than nothing," Ivy said with a sheepish shrug.

"There's nothing you could do about the aether core being small," Ruth told her. "You did as good a job as I could have."

Ivy grinned as they got up to leave.

"Alright, Michel, lead the way."

They wandered for what felt like hours, and Ruth couldn't help but glance to the sky line every few moments. The sun was about half way through setting and she wondered if Captain Hall and his men were at the factory yet. Of course, if they were, she wondered what they would make of the situation. Would they ascertain that she and Ivy had escaped, or would they think that they were dead? No one else had perished, to their knowledge, so it was entirely possible that they would figure out that they were alive, but it also stood to reason that they would know that the man in charge had also made it out. And that he had Ruth's plans. Ruth doubted that they would be subtle if they got to him first, and then she wouldn't have proof that she wasn't the traitor. She doubted Queen Victoria would take her at her word.

"Are we close yet?" Ruth heard Ivy ask, drawing her attention back from the skyline.

"I think I have an idea of which direction we should be heading," Michel said as he turned a corner. "Actually no, wait just a moment," he added about halfway down that street, taking another turn.

"Right, this way," he continued once they were a sufficient way down the next alley. "I am certain I have it now."

Ruth gave an unsure raise of her eyebrow, but Ivy followed along quite happily.

After zig-zagging through several more Paris streets, earning more than a few stares for their state of dress and Michel's obvious inhuman qualities, they reached a hotel.

"In here, I think," Michel said.

"They're not going to let us in the front door," Ruth muttered, wondering what exactly to do. They looked like the most common of people and they had no money to hand. There was no way such a nice establishment would even tolerate them in the lobby.

"Then we don't go in the front door," Ivy said, moving around the side of the building.

Ruth and Michel followed close behind as she led them to a side entrance. They slipped in fairly easily, finding themselves in the kitchen.

One of the chefs yelled something in French, which Ivy responded to with more yelling. They went back and forth for a few moments, and Ruth was sure that they were about to be kicked out, only for the chef to leave and Ivy to lead them up through to a set of maintenance stairs.

"His room is on the third floor," Ivy said as she led them up.

"And the chef just told you that?"

"I told him we were maintenance."

"And what was the yelling about?"

"The kitchen was noisy. Also, he didn't like us trudging through it."

"But not enough to kick us out?"

"He may not like it, but if we actually worked here and were late with repairs because of him, the boss would have had his head. So, he let us right through."

Ruth nodded, accepting Ivy's words.

"So, are we close to the spider?" Ruth asked Michel.

He shrugged. "I think so, but it is so difficult to tell with this small core."

"Well, hopefully he's still in his room. Or, at least, your plans are."

Ivy nodded as they reached the right room.

Michel pushed at the door, right where the lock was, fracturing the wood around it so that it opened.

"Who's there?" a voice called. It sounded young, not like the man in charge at all.

As they opened the door, Ruth saw a man standing in the middle of the room. On the bed next to him was the briefcase that the man in charge had been carrying. The man in the centre of the room was short and skinny, with freckles all over his face that were partially covered by his ginger-brown hair. Ruth actually felt kind of bad about scaring him, even if he was in possession of her plans.

"You're her!" he said, seemingly shocked. "He said you wouldn't come…"

Michel strode over to the boy and grabbed a hold of his shirt before effortlessly lifting him off the ground.

The boy whimpered as he started to cry and Michel seemed a little startled by the reaction.

"Put him down," Ruth said gently. "He's not going anywhere."

Michel did as he was asked, placing the boy down on the bed as Ruth took the briefcase for herself. She opened it to see her plans. Or, rather, what was left of them. Her little spider seemed to be doing a rather good job of tearing them up.

"Does everything you build eventually develop a mind of its own?" Ivy asked as she watched the spider crawl into Ruth's hand.

"I don't know, but this is truly becoming fascinating."

They turned their attention back to the boy.

"What's your name?" Ruth asked him.

"Jean."

"Jean, can you tell me if these were these the only copy of the plans?"

The boy shook his head. "There were others in the office at the factory."

"Taken care of," Ruth told him. "Any more?"

He shook his head.

"So, who is he? Your employer?" Ruth asked.

The boy shook his head again, this time harder. "I can't, Miss. Please. He'll kill me."

Michel took a step towards him. "What makes you think we won't kill you?"

The boy whimpered once more.

Ivy stepped towards him, putting a hand on his shoulder. He flinched away but quickly relaxed as he realised that she had no intent of hurting him.

"Please," Ivy said. She indicated to Ruth. "These are her plans and he stole them. We just want to make sure he can't do any harm with them."

"You've already destroyed the plans," the boy said. "He'll probably kill me for that alone…"

"Then help us to arrest him. He won't be able to hurt you then."

The boy looked at Ivy before turning to Ruth, seemingly examining them for any signs of deceit.

"It would be a shame for you to get hurt over this," Ruth told him, hoping to reassure. "I want to make sure that doesn't happen."

He nodded. "His name is Mr Banks. He never gave a first name. I know he worked with others, but I never knew their names, either."

Ruth sighed. "Well, hopefully Captain Hall will be able to make use of that information."

"Should we wait for Mr Banks to return?" Michel asked. "I assume he would be back for the briefcase and boy. We can arrest him then."

"I'm not sure it's a legal arrest when we're on foreign soil without permission," Ivy said under her breath so that only Ruth could hear her.

"I would rather avoid the word 'kidnap', though," Ruth explained.

"I see your point."

Ruth turned her attention back to Michel. "Yes, we should wait here to arrest him. It will make for quite the surprise, I should think."

Just as they were about to settle in to wait, they heard a large crash below them, followed by the sound of dozens of boots on wood.

Ruth sighed. "A pound says that's Captain Hall."

"There's no way I'm taking that bet," Ivy told her as the aforementioned boots arrived on their floor.

"Secure the area," she heard Captain Hall yell just before he made an appearance at the door.

"Lady Chapelstone?" he asked as he peered inside the room. "Where's Mr Banks?"

"He left. We were waiting to apprehend him when he got back. How did you know to come here? Or that Mr Banks was running this whole operation, for that matter?"

"We interrogated one of the factory workers."

Ruth sighed, pinching the bridge of her nose as she decided that she probably didn't want to know what that interrogation had entailed.

"Well, I don't suppose he would be fool enough to return now that the hotel is occupied," Ruth said as she folded her arms. "We have destroyed all copies of the plan, however. Now its only location is here." She pointed to her temple.

"Unless he memorised it."

Ruth shrugged. "Given that he couldn't figure out how to upgrade the design, I highly doubt that."

"Does this mean we can go home?" Ivy asked.

Ruth turned to Captain Hall and gave him a pointed look.

"I still want to sweep the city for this Mr Banks."

"And risk being seen? The occupation of this hotel has probably already alerted the local authorities to our presence."

Jean stepped forward. "I... I know where he usually goes in town. I could take you to the different places to look for him."

Captain Hall nodded. "I will accompany you on my own, then. That shouldn't draw any more attention." He turned back to Ruth. "I shall attempt to be swift in my search. I want to be on the way back to London by sunrise. You and the others should head back to the airship and wait for my return. Thomas has been worrying over you."

Ruth nodded with a slight smile before leaving the room, Ivy and Michel following close behind.

"Hear that?" Ivy asked. "They're on a first-name basis now."

Ruth just smiled, her words having left her in the wave of exhaustion that had swept over her mind.

15

The trip back to London was a fairly uneventful one, though it solidified Ruth's hatred of air travel. Ivy and Michel kept her company in her room as she did her best to keep her breakfast down.

"What do you think Thomas is doing right now?" Ivy sang in a way that insinuated that he was enjoying Captain Hall's company.

"I'm sure I don't want to know," Ruth told her as she watched intently out of the window, hoping that it would settle her stomach. Unfortunately, it did little to help.

"I'm more concerned about the fact that Mr Banks got away," Michel said.

Ruth sighed, turning to him only to see a disconcerted look on his face that she had never seen before.

"He doesn't have the plans," Ruth reasoned. "It's unlikely that he'll be able to restart his operations."

"Do you honestly think that will stop him?" Michel asked. "He not only got a look at those plans, he also knows about your disrupter, which is a much simpler design."

Ivy moved over to him, placing a comforting hand on his shoulder. "Michel, trust us when we say that we won't let anything happen to you. And, if he does start up his operations again, we'll stop him. We promise."

"So," Queen Victoria said, staring Ruth down in that way that shook her to her core.

It took all of her strength to keep her gaze.

"You let this Mr Banks escape?"

Thankfully, Captain Hall stepped forward at that. "Ma'am, he escaped the city before we could apprehend him, but he no longer has the plans. It's doubtful that he could cause us any more problems."

She regarded them both for a moment before nodding. "I shall have an eye kept out for any future trouble, but it seems that you have done an adequate job for now." She turned to give Ruth a particularly stern look. "I think that any of your unused plans would be safer under my protection, don't you?"

Ruth's stomach clenched at that. Her unused plans remained unused for a reason. Plans that had potential military use - uses that could result in devastation - weren't something she was happy to put in anyone else's hands.

But then, after this incident, she couldn't really say that they were much safer with her.

The thought occurred to her that she could destroy them, much like she had destroyed those for the mechanical men, but that thought made her blood run cold. She told herself that she would never be able to forgive herself if she destroyed those plans and then they became necessary, but, in all honesty, she couldn't deny that pride played a small part in it.

"I'll have them brought here right away," Ruth agreed, ignoring the churning of her stomach telling her that she was making a grave mistake.

L.C. Mawson

BOOK THREE
LADY RUTH AND THE AMERICAN ESCAPADE

1

Ruth stepped away from her workbench to be greeted by an all-too-familiar sound.

Silence.

Of course, it was never truly silent in London. That was impossible. No, she could hear the sound of people in the streets, along with the mechanical clacking of machines, some of which she was most likely responsible for.

No, it was never truly silent in her townhouse, but it was still eerily so. The sound of people outside could never, after all, replace the sound of people within the walls.

When Ruth was young, she had imagined that she would love to live alone. It seemed the perfect solution to her difficulty with people, but now it simply left her alone with her thoughts for far too long, which was its own special kind of torture.

Thomas had been the first to go. Ruth had expected it sooner or later. He couldn't remain a bachelor forever, she had told herself before she had known that his tastes lay with other men. After that, she had assumed that he would get bored of nannying her at some point. In the end, both of her suspicions had come to pass. He had fallen for

Captain Hall, the man who had been in charge of keeping an eye on Ruth when she was suspected of treason.

Thomas had started following Hall on his missions a few years ago, pretending to be some kind of consultant, and Ruth had seen little of him after that.

Then had been Michel. The mechanical man she had constructed, who had inexplicably gained sentience. Despite being made of metal, he wasn't mechanically minded himself. While Ivy and Ruth had spent their days on their projects in the workshops, he had read every book they had available. And then he had read any he could get his hands on.

In the end, Ruth had been the one to approach him about getting a more formal education. With his incredible intellect, and the unique opportunity he posed, it wasn't difficult to get Oxford to take him.

So, that was Michel out of the nest.

Last to leave had been Ivy, to Ruth's surprise. Ivy had been her student, and Ruth had thought that she would leave much sooner. She had been a quick study and had ambitions of her own, and yet she had stayed.

Ruth had started to feel guilty about that after a time. She felt as if Ivy was only staying out of pity for her, and she didn't want to hold the young woman back like that. Not when she had so much potential. So, Ruth had talked to Ivy about potential future ambitions and had eventually arranged to have her work as an airship designer for the Crown.

Which just left Ruth. All alone, just as she had always wanted, and yet far lonelier than she had ever anticipated.

Her thoughts were interrupted by a knock at the door, perking her up as she remembered that it was time for Michel's monthly check-up. She rarely saw him between the visits on the last of the month, so she cherished them whenever they came.

"Michel," she greeted as she opened the door.

"Ruth," he greeted with a smile that looked as human as possible with small ceramic plates instead of skin. "I see you haven't hired any servants for the house."

She ignored the suggestion for what felt like the thousandth time. It was always the same suggestion from either him or Ivy. While Ruth would readily admit that she was too absentminded to keep the house in good condition, she didn't want to invite strangers into her home. No, it was better to do without, reputation, mess and loneliness be damned.

"Follow me," she said, leading him up to the workshop. "How are things? How is Oxford?"

"It is pleasant enough."

"Still making friends?"

"No, I feel I have made the appropriate amount now. However, I am retaining the current ones."

"That's good. How are your studies going?" she asked as they entered the workshop and she brought out her tools.

Michel started to bare his chest without having to be asked. "Well. My professors are always impressed by my ability to retain information, though some make snide comments about me being more suited to sciences."

Ruth couldn't help but smile a little as she started to examine the inside of his chest. "Well, we both know how I feel about the arts."

"'A lot of pretentious old men who like to dictate the standards of culture to the rest of us', I believe was what you said last time we had this conversation."

"That is entirely possible." She gave a hum as she finished up her inspection. "Well, there's a little wear, but nothing that needs to be addressed right now. I'll make a note to look again next month. Is there anything specific that has been troubling you that you would like me to take a look at?"

Michel looked away awkwardly at that. "I... I have been wondering if my aether core might be malfunctioning."

Ruth frowned. It had looked fine to her. But she got out her aether detector anyway, moving it over his chest.

"The readings look fine to me," she said. "And, if it was, the secondary core would kick in to compensate. What makes you think it's malfunctioning?"

"It feels as if there are occasional... disruptions to the flow of energy."

"The secondary core should definitely be compensating for anything like that. Is anything causing it? Does it happen around any other aether-powered devices? It could be interference..."

"I... No. I don't think Ivy carries aether-powered devices on her."

Ruth's eyebrows shot up into her hair. "Ivy? This happens every time Ivy is around?"

"Yes. What do you think it means?"

Ruth folded her arms. "Well, if you were made of flesh and your heart skipped a beat every time you saw a specific person, I would suggest that you might have romantic feelings towards the person."

Michel looked decidedly like a man who had been told something he already knew and was trying to avoid.

Ruth smiled, though she couldn't help the hollow feeling in her chest. She had never particularly wanted romantic feelings towards anyone, but knowing that

Michel also wouldn't have those feelings had always made her feel less alone.

"You're in love with Ivy," she said, hoping to prompt him into talking about it. It was clearly bothering him a great deal.

"Yes," he eventually managed, his voice barely more than a whisper. "I think that I am."

"Well, that's wonderful. Have you told her?"

"Of course not! I'm just made of metal and she… She should have someone real."

"You are real," Ruth countered. "You're as real as any flesh and blood man. It is perfectly possible that she returns your feelings."

"Possible, but highly improbable, and I would rather not put her in the awkward position of rejecting me."

"Michel…"

"You're using the mothering tone."

Ruth folded her arms at that. The damn mech always knew how to shut her up. "Fine. Be like that. I just want you to be happy."

"I know, Ruth, but being rejected by Ivy won't make me happy." He took out his pocket-watch. "I'm afraid, if that is all, I have to go. Some friends accompanied me to London and we're going out."

"Well, you're fine as far as I can see, but feel free to pop back if you experience any difficulties between now and next month, or if your core problems get any worse."

He nodded. "Thank you."

"It's no trouble. Have fun with your friends."

"You are, of course, free to come with me," he said. "I'm sure my friend would love to meet the legendary Owl."

Ruth smirked at the old name. "Perhaps, but I think I'm a little old to be out at the pub with students."

"Nonsense."

She raised an eyebrow.

"Oh, well, I suppose you're right. I'm just worried about you. You're here all alone now that Ivy's gone."

She smiled. "Michel, I am perfectly fine. Now, go on. You'll be late."

As soon as the door shut behind him, Ruth found herself greeted by the oppressive silence once more.

She made her way to the kitchen and let the kettle boil as she read through a new paper on the potential applications of mechanical minds (which, as usual, made a few snide remarks about her for keeping the information to herself). She brewed herself some tea and drank as she continued to read.

Once the kettle was empty, she decided to call it a night, making her way to bed, despite the relatively early hour.

2

Ruth was awoken much earlier than she would have liked by the sound of someone knocking on her door.

She pulled on her dressing gown, cursing the lack of servants. Of course, she would hate them the rest of the time, but for callers before she was decent, they would have been a blessing.

She yanked the door open, hoping that it was someone she knew, only to be surprised to see Michel and Ivy standing there.

"Oh, I didn't think about you not being up yet," Ivy said as she noted Ruth's state of undress.

Ruth shook her head, simply glad to see her former student. "It's no trouble. Come on in. What can I do for you two?"

"Well, we thought we would see if you were free for lunch," Ivy explained as she and Michel entered the house. "It is almost noon…"

Ruth nodded. "Of course. Just give me a moment to change."

Ruth hurried to put on her easiest dress, wanting to make herself look presentable without making Ivy and Michel wait for too long.

As she left her room, she ran straight into Michel.

"Where's Ivy?" Ruth asked.

"She's still downstairs. I wanted to talk to you about, well, about what we talked about yesterday," he said in a hushed voice.

"Oh, yes. Have you told her how you feel?"

"No. No, no, not at all. But I was thinking… Perhaps if, instead of these ceramic plates, I had something that looked more like real skin, so that I looked far more like a human man, I think I might have an easier time confessing my feelings."

Ruth sighed, folding her arms. "I suppose such a thing may be possible but, Michel, I do want you to think about this. It would be a drastic change and would most likely change how you function on a day-to-day basis."

"But you think it can be done?"

"I'm really not sure."

"If anyone can figure it out, it's you."

"Michel, you're not listening to me."

"I have perfect hearing."

"Then you are choosing to ignore my point. Michel, if you make such a drastic change, you have to be sure that you're doing it for you, not for Ivy or anyone else."

"But you make upgrades to me all the time. Why is this different?"

"Michel, have I ever made an upgrade to you that I didn't ask you about before?"

"No, I suppose not."

"And I have never pursued an upgrade that you thought was irrelevant. So, I want to know that you want this for you before I do it, not that you think it will impress Ivy. Not least because I am not convinced of that fact."

"But if I still want it after thinking about it, you'll do it?"

"Yes. Come back to me with your decision in a few days and, in the meantime, I will look into how viable it is."

"Thank you."

"Come on, Ivy has been waiting long enough."

Ruth definitely got the feeling that Ivy and Michel had only visited her out of pity but, as they finished up their lunch, she decided that she was happier about having seen them than she was annoyed.

"So," her former student said as they headed back to Ruth's, "what projects have you been working on?"

"Nothing too exciting, I suppose. Recently, I've been spending a lot of time making sure that no one else is close to replicating Michel. Other than that, all I've done is improve upon the spider designs for better mobility."

"Would you mind showing me? I miss talking to you about your designs."

Ruth sighed, looking to see that Michel was walking quite a way ahead of them. "Of course you can, but I have to ask, this visit of yours was rather unexpected…"

Ivy looked sheepish. "That obvious, huh?"

"A little."

"Okay, well, I was out with Michel and a few of his student friends last night and Michel mentioned that he was a little worried about you. He said that you don't get many visitors and you don't leave the house much."

"If I wanted to leave the house, I would."

"I know, but that doesn't mean that you don't miss people."

Ruth sighed as they reached her house. "I suppose it has been a little lonely as of late."

"I'm sorry I've not been around more," Ivy said as they entered the house. "I haven't been avoiding you. I've just been busy."

"Ivy, I don't expect you to keep me company. You have your own life to be getting on with."

Almost as soon as the door shut behind them, there was a knock.

Ruth frowned as she opened it, only to reveal Thomas and Captain Hall standing on the other side.

She sighed, turning to Ivy. "You know, if you were going to organise a party, it would have been nice to know ahead of time."

"Ruth, we need to talk," Captain Hall said as she turned back to him, his serious tone telling her that he wasn't there at Ivy's request at all.

"Come on in," Ruth said, letting them through.

It felt odd to have Captain Hall in her house. When Thomas had still lived there, he had refrained from bringing him home. Captain Hall and Ruth's relationship had never quite got past the brief time she was considered a potential traitor and he had been in charge of watching over her.

"What can I do for you?" she asked once they joined the others.

"I have received some troubling news from a friend of mine," Thomas said as he folded his arms. "It seems that more mechanical men have surfaced in America."

"More mechanical men? But no one has the plans; we made sure of that," Ruth protested.

"We know," Captain Hall said, "but we suspect Mr Banks is up to his old tricks again."

"So he's trying to frame me once more?"

"I doubt framing you was his original intent, but we do suspect that he is the one building the mechanical men."

"Does anyone else know?"

Thomas shook his head. "The Queen hasn't been informed, if that's what you're asking. I think I'm one of the few with the information in the country, and I came straight to you."

Ruth couldn't help but wonder if Hall had protested that, but she pushed the thought aside. "So, what do we do?"

"We can take my airship to investigate," Captain Hall told her. "I have license to act of my own discretion on occasion, so we needn't tell anyone."

Ruth nodded. "When do we leave?"

"At dawn tomorrow. I do not wish to dally. If the Queen finds out that we knew and kept it from her…"

"If she finds out at all, I'm a dead woman."

Ivy stepped forward. "We'll come too. Won't we, Michel?"

"Of course. I want to stop them from using my brothers for nefarious purposes as much as anyone."

"And I could use some time in the air to see my designs in action."

"You don't have to-" Ruth started, but Ivy cut her off.

"We know that, but we have our own reasons."

Ruth nodded, deciding to just accept that they were coming along. "Then I suppose we leave at dawn."

3

Ruth couldn't help but give a disgruntled groan as she boarded the airship. She hadn't been back in the air since their trip to France and was of the opinion that getting back aboard an airship at any point before she died would be too soon.

And yet, here she was, being assured that it was faster than travelling by sea. She knew that. Her designs had been the ones to make that the case. But it still didn't mean that she had to like travelling in such a nausea-inducing way.

"Are you alright? You look a little pale," Michel said.

"I'm fine," Ruth told him firmly, having had quite enough of his fussing over her. "Where's the rest of the crew?" she asked as they made their way onto the empty bridge. "What have they been told about our voyage?"

"There is no crew," Captain Hall informed her. "Thanks to Ivy here, the ship is entirely automated."

Ruth grinned, examining the instruments. "Truly?"

Ivy nodded, proceeding to show her all of the ways she had got the instruments to work in harmony with very little human input.

Ruth faded in and out of what she was saying, a little too distracted by the upsetting feeling of not being on the ground, but she was proud of Ivy regardless. The young girl had truly found her place in the world.

"I'm sorry," Ivy said, halting herself. "Here I am prattling on and you look positively ill."

Ruth shook her head. "I shall be fine. We will be in the air for a long time yet, after all."

"Actually, there's medicine for that."

"For illness caused by travel?"

"Well, sort of. Captain Hall has it."

"Ah yes," Hall said, passing over a small vial. "It is designed to keep you in a deep sleep for the entire journey. You will go to sleep in London and wake up when we reach America."

Ruth gave the vial a dubious look. "I don't know, Captain. This sounds like nothing more than a way for you to get me out of your hair." She remembered to smile to indicate that she was joking.

"Two birds with one stone," he replied with a smile of his own.

She sighed. "I'm sure I'll be fine, Captain, but thank you for the offer."

She downed the contents of the vial not more than five minutes later.

Ruth awoke, wondering if the vial had worked. Were they truly in America already?

Her thoughts were interrupted by a loud screeching noise, quickly followed by an explosion that rocked the ship.

Just as she pulled herself over the side of her bed, Michel and Ivy hurried into her room.

"Oh good!" Ivy said. "You're already up. And dressed. How long have you been up?"

"She took the medication while still clothed," Michel reminded her.

Ruth grumbled a little at that decision as her dress had poked into various points, leaving them quite sore.

"What's going on?" Ruth asked.

"Well, we reached America, but we were immediately accosted by pirates not more than a mile from shore," Ivy informed her.

"Pirates? You mean in sea-faring ships?"

"No, airships. We have to get off the ship. It won't be able to take much more damage."

"Lead the way," Ruth said.

Ivy took them out into the corridor and around the corner, only to run straight into the pirates in question.

The pirates trapped them in place, sneering at them.

"That the only crew?" one of the pirates asked.

Another shook their head. "These don't look like crew. Passengers, I'd reckon."

The first one took their pistol and aimed it at Ivy. "Where's the crew?"

"There aren't any. The ship is automated."

"Auto-what?"

"It doesn't need a crew. It runs itself."

The pirate looked at her as if she had told him that it ran on magic, but Ruth soon realised that the shocked expression had less to do with what Ivy had said, and more with the bullet wound in his chest.

He dropped to the floor, quickly followed by his crewmates, to reveal Thomas standing behind him with a gun.

"When did you get so good with that thing?" Captain Hall asked with a sly grin.

"Amazingly, I do sometimes listen when you try and teach me things."

"I should give you a gun more often..."

Thomas replied with a grin and Ruth decided that time was too short not to interrupt them.

"Now that we're all together, how are we getting off this thing?" she asked them.

"There's a small scouting craft," Hall told her. "If we can get to it, we can make it to the mainland."

Ruth nodded as Hall led the way down to the scout craft.

They only saw a few more of the pirates on their way, which Hall and Thomas made quick work of, but the way the ship continued to shake with explosions told them that there were many more outside.

"Once we're in the scout craft, what's to stop the pirates from simply shooting us down?" Ruth asked. "Surely it's less able to withstand bombardment than this ship."

Hall shook his head. "Perhaps, but it's a much smaller target. Chances are, they won't be able to hit it."

Ruth gave a hum of agreement, though she wasn't completely onboard with that reasoning. Nonetheless, it was either the scout craft or go down with the ship.

They quickly made it to the scout craft and all piled in, squishing up against each other as Hall struggled to reach the controls. The craft was clearly not designed for more than three people.

They managed to launch the craft, however, gliding down and away from the airship, just in time to see it rocked by another explosion and losing altitude.

Ruth watched, waiting for the pirate ships to realise that they had escaped, but she instead saw a handful of smaller craft arriving, all with the American flag on the side of them.

"Looks like the authorities finally saw fit to intervene," Thomas said as they landed the ship on the beach.

They scrambled out of it, Ruth thanking God for her return to solid land. After that ordeal, she felt that she needed a cup of tea and a long sleep, but she steeled herself, knowing that neither were likely.

One of the American ships followed them down within a minute or two, for which Ruth was glad. She wasn't exactly sure how they were supposed to go about their mission without their ship. Or anything else, for that matter, besides the clothes on their backs. And the escape craft, she supposed, as her mind tried to suppress everything that had happened by focusing on practicality. She wondered just how much they could get for it. Would it be enough to get passage back to England?

Captain Hall straightened his uniform jacket as the pilot got out of the American craft and made his way to them.

"Looks like you lot got yourselves into quite the mess," the pilot said as he approached with a smile. "Are you the only survivors?"

"The only passengers," Captain Hall said. "We were flying a Thames V7. It was all fully automated."

"That's a British ship, is it not?"

"Correct. I'm Captain Hall and this is my crew."

"Here on the Queen's orders?"

"I'm not at liberty to discuss that with anyone but your higher-ups."

The pilot seemed a little put-out by that, but quickly perked back up. "Well, we were on our way to the capital when we noticed your predicament. We'd be happy enough to bring you along."

"That would be much appreciated."

Ruth raised an eyebrow as they went to follow the pilot, wondering just what exactly Hall was playing at, but she kept her mouth shut for fear of shattering their ruse.

4

They arrived at the American capital within a few hours, which Ruth was quite impressed by. She knew that her designs had been worked into smaller, faster craft, but she had yet to see one in person. It was quite a bit kinder on her stomach as well.

"There it is," the pilot said, puffing his chest out with pride. "The White House. I bet you folks don't have anything like that in England."

"There's Buckingham Palace," Ruth pointed out. "So, is that where we're headed? The White House?"

The pilot shrugged. "Depends on how far up the chain of command you meant before."

"The White House should be fine," Captain Hall said. "We are, after all, here on the orders of Her Majesty."

"Do you intend to speak with the presidents?" the pilot asked excitedly.

"Presidents?" Ivy asked. "I thought there was only one president?"

"Not for the past year or so, since the Council was built."

"I suppose who we speak to will be up to your more direct superiors," Captain Hall said and the pilot nodded as he landed the craft.

As they left the craft, Ruth took the time to inspect it, finding that the underside was covered in balloons, which must have been what kept them in the air, with large aether tanks. She supposed that the tanks must keep the air within heated in order to ascend. There were another two aether tanks on the back that seemed to power two large propellers, which were able to move along the rear end of the ship and to the sides. She supposed they must be in charge of the direction of the ship.

She was pulled from her inspection by a man in a rather crisp looking uniform approaching.

"Harrison," he said to the pilot in a gruff voice, his rather impressive moustache moving as he spoke, "what have you managed to drag back this time, you overgrown cat?"

Hall grinned at the man. "Fredrickson! It's been too long."

"Hall!" the man responded. "You're damn right it has. What are you doing this side of the globe?"

"I'm here on business for Her Majesty. Our airship was accosted by pirates. Your fine men drove them off, but we were unable to save the ship. So, here I am, with a handful of VIPs, no ship, and with a mission to complete."

Fredrickson nodded in understanding. "Well, of course, any help I can give is yours. Mind telling me a few details of your mission?"

Hall indicated to Ruth. "This is The Owl."

"The inventor?"

"The very same. She has been sent here because of rumours that you have developed your own mechs."

"You mean the automatons?"

"The mechanical men."

"Yeah, they're called automatons out here. Well, I suppose if that's your mission, you'd better speak to the Council."

"Your pilot mentioned them. Who are the Council?"

"The Council of Presidents. The president himself is out of town, so they're the best to speak to."

Hall nodded, silently following Fredrickson as he led them inside the White House. Ruth desperately wanted to ask what exactly this Council was, but she left it be. She didn't want to risk putting her foot in her mouth.

Of course, that thought immediately fled her mind as she was led to a room filled with mechanical men. They were all dressed in various out-of-fashion clothes, with more than a few sporting old-fashioned white wigs, including the one in the middle, who was slightly elevated above the rest. He also, for some inexplicable reason, given that the rest of him was made of metal, appeared to have wooden teeth.

"This is the Council?" Ivy asked.

Fredrickson nodded. "When a former president died, their brains were kept preserved in the hope that there would one day be a way to revive them."

"And I thought royalty were weird," Ruth muttered.

Thomas folded his arms. "Quite. Wasn't the whole point of the presidency that no one person would rule forever? This seems quite contrary to that wish."

"The Council don't rule," Fredrickson told them. "The preservation process wasn't nearly good enough for that. No, they simply advise."

Ivy moved a little closer to Michel. "Just as long as none of them try to claim me as their property or anything."

The mech - or automaton, Ruth supposed - with wooden teeth spoke up in a particularly grating shout. "WHO ADDRESSES THE COUNCIL?" it demanded.

Fredrickson stepped forward. "The Owl. She is the inventor responsible for automatons."

They all immediately spun their heads around to her in eerie synchronised movements.

"YOU ARE THE MOTHER OF AUTOMATONS?"

Ruth sighed. That name was a new - and unwelcome - one. "Yes, I suppose, if you want. I'm here to see how automatons have been used in America."

"WHY?"

"Curiosity," she lied.

"YOU CAN SEE BEFORE YOU HOW WE ARE USED."

"How about the production process? How were you built?"

"WE DO NOT KNOW. THESE BODIES WERE CONSTRUCTED BY A PRIVATE COMPANY."

"And you didn't think to ask about how the bodies you are now using were constructed?"

"IT WAS NOT RELEVANT. NOT WHEN IT WAS THE ONLY WAY TO PROCURE SUCH BODIES."

Ruth sighed. Even the automatons were mad at her for keeping her plans to herself.

"Can you at least tell us the name of the company who manufactured you?"

The automaton closest to her rolled up its sleeve to show her the brand on its right arm.

WESTTECH, the brand proclaimed.

"IS THERE ANYTHING ELSE?" the head automaton, which Ruth had just realised was probably meant to be George Washington, asked.

"No," Captain Hall replied for her. "Thank you."

They left quickly, feeling defeated.

"Well, that was pointless," Ruth declared.

"We got the name of the company producing them," Michel pointed out.

"Yes, but nothing else. We don't even know where to find this WestTech facility. Not to mention, they're already using my designs for ridiculous purposes."

Ivy nodded with a shudder. "Dead slave owners should stay dead. I'm not going to sleep for a month."

Michel responded by offering her a comforting hand, which she took.

"There has to be some way to figure out where WestTech is," Thomas figured.

Ivy perked up a little, seemingly spotting something down the hallway. "Perhaps we're asking the wrong person."

She bounded down the hall after a man with even darker skin than hers. He had flecks of white in his otherwise short black hair and a toolbox, and was wearing a brown jumpsuit.

"Excuse me, are you one of the mechanics who works on the Council?" Ivy asked him.

"I am indeed. Jonathan Smith, at your service. And you are?"

"Ivy Miller." She turned to introduce Ruth, but the man was already shaking her hand.

"The inventor of the automated airship system?"

She nodded, seemingly dumbstruck.

"My daughter is a huge fan of yours. She saw you in a newspaper and has wanted to be an inventor ever since."

"Oh. Well... I'm flattered."

"But never mind me, you were asking about the Council?"

"Yes, we were wondering about their construction and operation. Specifically, we were wondering where to find the WestTech facility. We wish to speak with the owners about a tour."

"Well, I'm not sure about the location of the facility, but I do have all of the WestTech manuals at my home. You're more than welcome to come and have a look over them."

"Thank you. Would it be alright if my mentor came as well? She's the one who invented the automatons in the first place."

He nodded. "Sure, that's no problem."

Captain Hall spoke up at that. "We'll take Michel with us and will try to get our bearings."

Ruth nodded. "We'll meet you back here at sunset."

5

Jonathan's home was a relatively modest one in a section of town that seemed predominantly occupied by black residents.

"Honey, you'll never guess who I met at work," he said as he entered the house, Ivy following close behind and Ruth trailing a bit, feeling like an interloper.

"You've not brought home strays again, have you?" a tired voice asked from further in the house. The owner of the voice walked to the front door, a little girl trailing behind her. The voice belonged to a woman who seemed only a year or two older than Ruth at most, with an hourglass figure to rival hers as well; however, her skin was much closer to Ivy's dark tones, if not darker, and her hair was tied back in small braids. Or, at least, braids were the closest thing Ruth could name to the style. She liked it. It seemed practical in the way she often wished British fashions were.

The young girl beside her gasped as she saw Ivy. "You're Ivy Miller!" she exclaimed, bounding up to her.

The woman folded her arms with a disbelieving look.

"Yes, I am," Ivy confirmed as she lifted the little girl up into her arms. "Your dad told me that you like my work."

The girl nodded. "I've been building my own things out of spare parts. Do you want to see?"

Ivy looked to the girl's mother, who gave a nod of approval.

"I would love to," Ivy told the girl before being taken away.

Jonathan turned to Ruth. "And this is The Owl. She wanted to have a look at my instruction manuals for the automatons."

"And you couldn't get them anywhere else?" the woman asked. "WestTech, for example?"

"I'm not sure that they would be all that welcoming of me," Ruth admitted. "I never gave them permission to work from my plans."

The woman sighed, turning back to her husband. "You'll never stop bringing trouble home with you, will you?"

He gave an impish grin. "Now where would the fun be in that?"

She shook her head with a smile. "Go on, then. Go get the manuals. I'll make us all some tea." She turned to Ruth as Jonathan headed to another room. "You do like tea, don't you?"

"I do, but I thought Americans didn't. Something about preferring to throw it in the sea."

The woman laughed. "Perhaps a hundred years ago. Now, I'm quite fond of it. Oh, where are my manners? I'm Imani."

"Ruth."

"Well, Ruth, how about we make our way to the kitchen, and you can tell me why you're here in person."

"I beg your pardon?"

"I'm not a fool," Imani said as they made their way through to the kitchen. "You're a wealthy woman, and last I heard, The Owl worked for the Queen of England. You have the resources at your disposal to send any number of lackeys across the ocean to investigate. Why come yourself?"

Ruth shrugged. "I like to do things myself."

"And you like telling half-truths, apparently."

Ruth sighed. "Fine. If this problem gets back to the Queen, she may think I sold the designs. Given that I have stopped her from using them, that would either end in her executing me for treason or deciding that it was reason enough for her to use the designs herself. Neither of which are situations I particularly want to play out."

Imani narrowed her eyes at Ruth. "And you've gone and embroiled my husband in this?"

"All I did was ask to see his instruction manuals. He can't be bothered over that."

"There is very little that the authorities wouldn't see fit to bother a black man over."

Ruth frowned. That hadn't even occurred to her. "I promise, we won't tell anyone we were here."

Imani regarded her carefully for a moment, before seemingly taking her at her word. "So," she started as she set about putting the kettle on, "did you and Ivy come here alone? Two unaccompanied women travelling so far from home... That seems like asking for trouble."

"No, we didn't. My uncle and his... friend came with us. As well as Michel."

"Michel?"

"The first mechanical man I built."

"I suppose it must be nice to have him about. No need for escorts when you built one yourself."

"Actually, I see little of him. He started university last year."

"And you don't have anyone at home? No husband?"

Ruth shrugged. "Never wanted one."

"You've never fallen in love?"

"No. And I don't think I ever will. I just don't think it's in me."

Imani smiled. "Me neither."

"Wait, but... You're married."

"Jonathan and I have been best friends for as long as I can remember. He fell in love with me, but I never had those feelings. Not for anyone. I told him as much, but we both wanted children, and he didn't seem to mind."

"So you got married anyway?"

"Yes."

"Huh... I guess I never had anyone I was close enough with to have that kind of arrangement. No men I wasn't related to, at any rate. Not to mention, most husbands would have tried to put a stop to my inventing."

Jonathan returned, his arms filled with heavy-looking books.

"These are the instruction manuals for the presidents," he said. "Each has their own, but there are only a few variations, so I only brought as many as I could carry."

"Thank you," Ruth said as she opened the first one, pouring over the pages as quickly as she could while still absorbing all of the information.

"These are rudimentary," Ruth declared after getting halfway through the first book. "Look at these designs. They're so inefficient."

"So they're not yours, then?" Jonathan asked.

Ruth shook her head. "Not my latest ones. No, it looks like they're working from my early plans. Or thereabouts. There are some variations, though they're poor ones."

"So then there's no problem," Imani said. "If they're not working from your designs, then it is simply a poor copy."

Ruth shook her head. "But the designs around the aether core are too similar. They're working from part of my design, that much is clear."

She shook her head, before turning back to Jonathan. "Are you sure you don't know where the WestTech facility is?"

He shook his head.

"What about spare parts? Surely you must get them from somewhere."

"They arrive periodically by train, but I don't know where the train comes from."

"No," Ruth agreed, "but someone at the station might..."

6

"You're sure these will fit?" Ruth asked as she eyed the new clothes Michel, Thomas and Hall had bought, since theirs had been lost when the ship went down.

"As sure as I can be," Michel told her.

Ruth nodded in acceptance as she huddled into herself. The train station was freezing, probably due to the late hour. At least that also meant that it was reasonably empty…

Thomas hurried back over to the huddled group from talking with one of the station workers.

"There's a late train leaving soon. It should head back to where the WestTech trains come from."

"Should?"

"Apparently WestTech is very secretive."

"But isn't that a safety problem? Shouldn't there be a record of where all of the trains come and go from?"

Thomas shrugged. "It seems the American government has made some concessions for WestTech in exchange for their technology."

Ruth folded her arms. "That seems like a terrible idea."

Hall snorted. "Ah yes, because you have certainly never wrangled concessions from the queen."

Ruth flushed. "That's different!"

"The only difference I see is that you think you're right."

"I *am* right."

"Which I suspect is exactly what the person running WestTech will say when we ask why they have been copying your designs."

Ivy stepped in. "Perhaps we should find this train, instead of bickering amongst ourselves."

After changing into one of her new dresses and settling down in her compartment, Ruth found herself once more confronted by just how much she hated to travel by train. It wasn't as terrible as air travel, or as arduous as travelling by carriage, but it still drained her of any energy.

A knock at the compartment door disrupted her turbulent thoughts.

"Come in," she called, wondering who it might be.

Michel entered, much to her relief. "May I sit with you?"

She nodded and he closed the door before sitting opposite her.

"I dislike trains," he told her. "They bother my internal spirit level."

"I am not fond of them either," Ruth agreed. "Is Ivy asleep?"

"No, I don't think so," he replied with a slight frown.

"Then what are you doing here?"

"Talking to you."

Ruth folded her arms. "I thought you were going to talk to Ivy about your feelings for her."

Michel shifted awkwardly at the reminded. "I've been putting it off until you can give me the upgrades we talked about."

Ruth sighed. "But what about the trip over here? Surely you talked to her then?"

"Not exactly. Not of anything important."

"Michel… This is more than a little ridiculous."

"I didn't want to tell her before I got the upgrades."

Ruth sighed. "And you're truly sure that you want them?"

Michel looked a little uneasy at that, telling her all she needed to know. She knew that he wouldn't want real skin once he thought through how inconvenient it would be. He was just using it as an excuse to delay telling Ivy about his feelings for her.

"Go and talk to Ivy," Ruth told him. "The worst she can do is tell you that she doesn't return your feelings."

Michel looked stricken.

Ruth sighed. "Even if she doesn't, it would be better if you knew. Otherwise you're just putting a strain on your friendship and making it even more likely that you might lose her."

Michel sighed. "You're right," he eventually said. "I should go and talk to her."

Ruth indicated to the door. Michel stood up and headed back down the corridor.

Ruth gave him a few moments before twisting her bracelet so that it unclasped from her wrist, unfolding into one of her mechanical spiders.

She took a small piece of metal from under its belly, which stayed attached via a small wire.

"Follow Michel," Ruth told the spider before putting the small piece of metal to her ear.

After a while, she heard a voice through the metal, telling her that the spider had arrived at Ivy's compartment.

"May I sit down?" she heard Michel ask.

"Of course," Ivy replied. *"It feels like too long since we've spoken."*

"It does, doesn't it? I'm sorry. I've been so busy with university that I've barely seen you lately."

"Well, it's not as if I've not also been busy. It's just strange that it feels as if we've barely talked when we've been travelling for so long. It almost feels as if... Well, pardon me for saying so, but it almost feels as if you have been avoiding me."

"I... There is some truth to that, I won't deny. I simply... I feared that our time apart had caused our friendship to wear. I'm not sure if I could handle that."

"Michel, I don't think such a thing is possible. Though I am sorry for us not spending more time together."

"As am I."

Silence settled in their compartment and Ruth sighed as the spider returned to her, seemingly realising that there was no more conversation to relay.

Ruth leaned back in her seat in an attempt to become more comfortable, hoping that she could manage some sleep during the journey. Her thoughts, however, stayed on Michel and Ivy. He may not have told her how he felt, Ruth thought to herself, but at least they were talking once more. That would have to be enough for now.

7

When the train finally reached its destination, Ruth was sure that it had broken down. There was barely anything within sight as she disembarked. Certainly, it was exaggerating to call it a town. Not to mention how temporary everything looked. The buildings seemed as if they might fall down in a heavy rain - a stark contrast to the stone structures that had stood on English soil for hundreds of years.

America's newness, she decided, was too strange to even feel real. How could land lack such a basic element as a sense of history? The capital had been different, but not by much. Here, it was too stark for her to ignore.

"It's not exactly London, is it?" Ivy asked as she looked around, squinting against the harsh sun.

Hall let out a snort. "My dear, it's not even Newcastle."

His love elbowed him for the derisive words about his hometown, though Thomas did chime in with, "It's barely Dinnington."

"Where?" Ivy asked.

"A mining village just north of Newcastle."

Ruth gave the buildings a quick once-over as she began to sweat beneath her heavy dress. She wished she had worn lighter clothing.

"Do you suppose that building is the pub?" she asked, gesturing at an establishment with swinging doors out front.

Hall nodded. "I would recognise a drinking establishment in any part of the world."

As they approached, they heard shouting from within, telling Ruth that this was indeed some kind of pub.

Before they could reach the door, someone flew backwards through them, landing with a sickening thud on the ground before them.

"I say!" Ruth exclaimed just as another figure followed him out.

It took Ruth a moment to realise that the newest arrival was, in fact, a woman, as she was wearing jeans and a shirt, a hat covering her hair.

The woman was walking backwards, her eyes on the door rather than the man on the ground behind her. Three more men spilled out of the establishment, making a beeline for her.

"This has been fun, boys," the woman said with an accent that Ruth found a little grating, "but I've got places to be."

The man at the forefront of the trio flushed bright red and lunged forward.

She side-stepped out of the way with seconds to spare, using the fact that he was caught off-guard to put him flat on his back as well.

"Do you really want to keep this up?" she asked the others.

The man on the left looked apprehensive, telling Ruth that he really didn't want to keep it up, but also didn't want to wound his pride by conceding a fight to a woman.

The man on the right had no such quandary, lunging for the woman as the first man had.

She side-stepped once more, but this man was ready for her. However, just as he was about to land a blow, the woman delivered one of her own with her boot, right between his legs.

Thomas and Hall tensed up beside Ruth as Ivy struggled to hold back a laugh.

"Last chance," the woman said to the third man, who scurried off after only a moment's thought.

"Good riddance," she muttered before turning to Ruth and the others. "Enjoy the show?"

Ruth was caught off-guard, but Michel stepped forward. "It was a fairly impressive one."

The girl shrugged, walking back into the pub. "I suppose. Now, if you'll excuse me, they interrupted my drink."

"Well, that was terrifying," Thomas said.

Ivy shrugged. "Well, we need information and she seems capable..."

Thomas shook his head violently. "Oh, no. Not her. I like everything in my trousers just the way it is, thank you very much."

Ivy rolled her eyes. "Men."

"I could speak to her," Michel offered. "She is unlikely to do me harm."

Ivy turned to Ruth. "Well, the other men are useless, you're not exactly our top negotiator, and I'm not going to feel comfortable talking to anyone in this small town until I see someone who isn't white."

Ruth nodded. "Michel it is. The rest of us will sit at a table inside."

They headed into the establishment and Michel went to the bar, which the woman from before was leaning against.

The others sat at a nearby table and Ruth inched her chair over so that she could hear exactly what was said.

"I was wondering if I may enquire after your assistance," Michel said to the woman.

She narrowed her eyes. "What is that accent? English?"

"Correct."

"I've never seen an English automaton before."

"Have you seen many of my kind?"

She shrugged. "A few. What's your designation?"

"I do not have a designation. I have a name. I am Michel."

"A name? So not an industrial model then. No, you're too pretty for that. The woman who looked like she had a bad smell under her nose, you're her servant automaton, aren't you?"

"I am no one's servant. Ruth is my friend."

The woman gave a disbelieving snort. "Alright, Michel. I'm Sally. What do you want?"

"We are new to the area and were wondering if you might have some information."

"About what?"

"We were led to believe that there was a WestTech facility out here..."

Sally froze. She turned back to Michel with a dark look in her eyes. "Look, I'm being real friendly here when I say this, but you need to get your mechanical behind out of town and never ask about WestTech again, you understand?"

"No, not especially."

"Then you're not as clever as the manufacturers have us believe."

She stormed out of the establishment at that, leaving behind a bewildered Michel.

He walked over to the others, sitting down next to them.

"Well, that could have gone better," he said.

Ruth sighed. "I wonder what caused that reaction. She looked almost scared."

"We can't leave," Ivy said. "But perhaps Michel should lay low until we know more."

Ruth nodded in agreement.

"I'll see about getting a room to stay in."

"Perhaps you should stay with him," Ruth said. "As you pointed out, this establishment is very white, and we may need someone on look-out if WestTech does track down Michel."

Ivy nodded. "I'll keep an eye on him."

"I don't need a nanny," Michel protested. "And Ivy will be in more danger if WestTech does come for me."

Ivy placed a comforting hand on his. "I know, Michel, but I will probably be of more use with you than down here."

He nodded reluctantly before following her to enquire about a room.

"This is getting us nowhere!" Thomas exclaimed, sitting back down next to Ruth and folding his arms. "No one wants to talk to us."

Hall gave a reluctant grunt of agreement. "It seems WestTech well and truly owns this town. Every time I ask about them, someone tenses up."

Ruth nodded, barely listening to them. In truth, she had done her best to talk to the strangers in the establishment, but it had been difficult, and she barely had the energy to move her eyes.

"You look like a shark," Hall told her.

"Pardon?" she asked, managing to just barely rouse herself.

"Your vacant expression, especially behind the eyes, is reminiscent of a shark."

She raised an eyebrow. "You truly know how to flatter a woman."

"Well, I can't say that flattering women was ever something I had an interest in."

Ruth gave a small smile before standing up. "If you'll excuse me, I think I need some fresh air."

"Be careful," Thomas warned. "It's getting dark out."

"I won't go far," she assured him. "The noise in here has become suffocating."

Thomas nodded as she headed out, seemingly accepting that she could take care of herself. She had her disrupter tied to a holster beneath her skirt, as always, so she had nothing to fear from WestTech automatons. Men who had imbibed a pint too many, however, would most likely give her more than a little trouble.

As soon as the dusk air hit her, Ruth felt her breathing ease. She truly hated crowded and noisy spaces.

She stood just outside the door for a few minutes, catching her breath, until she saw some men approaching. She suspected that many people would come and go within the next little while and she was directly in their way. While it meant that she was in public view, it also meant that she felt overly exposed.

She decided to head around the corner for a short walk, in the hopes that she would be ready to re-join Thomas and Hall once she returned.

The path was dusty, and Ruth worried over the state of the hem of her skirt. She didn't have many dresses to choose from, meaning that she couldn't afford to damage any of the ones she did have.

After a short while of wandering, she heard voices. Her hand instinctively moved to her skirt, pushing it down so she could ensure that her disrupter was still there.

She left it alone, however, when she recognised one of the voices as Sally's - only it wasn't speaking English.

Ruth crept up to the stable where the voices were coming from. She peered inside, doing her best to not be seen.

Inside was indeed Sally, laughing and talking with Indian woman. But not an Indian from India, which Ruth had always found incredibly confusing. Because, of course, people would rather continue referring to an entire people incorrectly than admit that a man made a mistake.

She supposed that meant that Sally was speaking Indian - or, rather, whatever language it was that these Indians spoke.

Sally said something that made the other woman laugh, and Sally blushed in turn. The other woman said something else, stepping closer to Sally before kissing her.

Ruth took that as her cue to leave, turning to head back to the pub - or saloon as she had since been informed by the bartender - only for her skirt to knock down a box of tools from atop a barrel.

Sally and her lover were in front of Ruth immediately. Sally aimed a pistol at her, while the other woman brandished a small weapon that Ruth couldn't even attempt to name. It looked sharp, though.

"You again?" Sally asked.

"You know her?" the other woman asked with an accent that was far less irritating than Sally's.

Sally nodded, putting away her pistol. Ruth didn't know whether to be relieved or insulted that she was thought of as so little a threat. The other woman kept her weapon up, soothing Ruth's ego slightly.

"She's a newcomer," Sally explained. "British. She and her friends came with an automaton in tow and started asking about WestTech."

"And you didn't tell me?"

"They're more likely to bring trouble than help, Chepi. We have no idea who they are or why they're here. We have no idea if they can actually help or if we should trust them."

"That's not true," Ruth interjected. "Well, the part about us bringing trouble isn't true. You were right about not knowing us."

"Really? You barge in here and just start asking about WestTech as if you've got a death wish and you honestly don't think you're bringing trouble right into town?" She turned back to her lover. "They have no idea what they're doing. If they want to get themselves killed, we shouldn't follow them."

Chepi mulled over Sally's words before turning to Ruth. "Why are you asking about WestTech?"

"I have my reasons."

Sally rolled her eyes. "I told you, she's of no help."

Ruth sighed. "Look, they stole something from me. I just want it back."

"Then you do it alone. You're of no use to us, so there's no reason why we should get involved with you." She turned away.

Chepi didn't follow. "How do you propose to get your stolen 'something' back?"

"I know technology inside and out," Ruth said, activating her bracelet so that it scuttled up her arm.

Sally raised her pistol, but relaxed when she realised what it was.

"Just show me where the facility is and I can retrieve my 'something' myself."

"I say we take her with us tomorrow," Chepi said. "She can probably be of some use."

"Fine," Sally sighed before turning back to Ruth. "We have our own issues with WestTech. We're going to scope out their facility tomorrow night. You can come with us, but if you take a single step out of line, I will shoot you - and I *don't miss*. Understood?"

Ruth nodded.

8

Despite fearing that Sally and Chepi would refuse to bring her with them, Ruth still brought Ivy with her to meet them the next night. She didn't want to be alone; she feared that the other women wouldn't be as quick to trust Thomas or Hall, and she didn't want to drag Michel into WestTech's path.

"She your servant?" Sally asked as the two arrived, her tone slightly mocking.

Ivy glared in response. "I'm her friend. Got a problem with that?"

Chepi stepped forward, placing a calming hand on Sally's arm. "Of course she doesn't. You two need to change into something more practical, however."

Ruth had worn her lightest dress. It was a deep blue and easier to move in than the rest of her wardrobe. She had also tied her hair up with a clip to keep it out of her way. Ivy wore a white shirt, with a black corset over the top, going under her breasts with straps over her shoulder. She also wore a black skirt which just brushed the ends of her boots, over the top of which was her toolbelt. Her hair was in its usual tie above her head.

However, looking at the other two, Ruth realised that they were, indeed, in far more practical attire. Sally dressed much like a man, in jeans and a brown shirt. She wore practical boots, and she had a jacket for the night air that Ruth imagined might feel chilly to someone not used to the temperatures of the north of England. Her blonde hair was tied back in a plait that she kept tucked under her wide-brimmed hat. Chepi wore a dress, but it only reached her knees. Beneath it she wore leggings and sensible boots. Her jet black hair was in two braids, decorated with beads.

"Let's get you some trousers," Sally said. "The last thing we need is one of you tripping over yourself."

"Trousers?" Ruth asked, shocked by the very notion. She was not always one to conform to the expectations of gender, she would admit, but there had to be a line somewhere.

Ivy smiled in a way that made Ruth think that someone had told her that Christmas had come early.

"It's trousers or stay behind," Sally told her.

Ruth sighed, folding her arms. "Then I suppose I shall have to suffer your wardrobe."

It wasn't long before Ivy had swapped out her skirt for a pair of jeans. Ruth had to change her entire outfit, sacrificing her dress for an incredibly tight pair of trousers and a shirt that was far too loose.

"This way to the facility," Sally told them, pointing over to the nearby woodlands.

"We're going on foot?" Ivy asked.

"We don't want the horses giving us away," Sally said as they began their otherwise silent trek.

Ruth, though usually fond of silence, found this particular brand to be rather oppressive. She itched to say something, to get the others talking, but nothing came to her. Every possible question that popped into her mind seemed either inane or invasive. Not to mention, if she started asking questions, she would be opening herself up to the same. The last thing she wanted was to end up having to reveal too much about herself to these relative strangers.

After so long that Ruth was sure the sun would rise at any moment, Chepi stopped dead, halting them all.

"It's just around here," she said. "We should split up. We can get a better look that way."

Sally nodded before turning to Ruth and Ivy. "I don't trust the two of you to go off together." She pointed to Ivy. "You come with me and your friend can go with Chepi."

Ivy rolled her eyes. "I have a name, you know."

Sally glared, then relented. "Ivy, you're with me."

Ivy nodded before following Sally in the opposite direction to Ruth and Chepi.

"Try to keep up," Chepi told her as she headed off with strong strides.

Ruth hurried a little to catch up, feeling a little out of breath. "Just because physical activity is not something I'm used to, doesn't mean that I'm useless."

"I never said that it did," Chepi replied, not bothering to look back at her. "But, for now, it is required."

Ruth nodded, deciding her keep her mouth shut as they moved towards the treeline. Ruth saw, just beyond, a large building which she assumed was a factory. It was easily three times the size of the facility she shut down in Paris.

"Why is it all the way out here?" Ruth asked. "It must have been difficult to build."

Chepi nodded. "I think it was so that people passing through the town wouldn't see it. They've gone to great lengths to keep their location quiet, if not secret."

"But why?"

"Why indeed, unless there is something about their operation that they wish to hide."

Ruth sighed, realising that they had probably been hiding from her. It was a relatively smart plan, she begrudgingly admitted. They worked to get a foothold in America without drawing attention from other parties across the world. By the time Ruth would have heard, if not for Hall, she would have been too late to do anything. Even arm England with her automatons.

"You know, don't you?" Chepi asked.

"Know what?"

"Why WestTech is hiding. When I said that they were, your face... You know exactly what they fear."

Ruth sighed, figuring that secrecy had hardly helped so far. "They fear me. I'm the original inventor of the automaton. Michel was my first and only attempt to build one. I didn't want the world to have access to my creation. I knew too many people would be hurt if they were ever turned to military use, so I didn't allow them to be. I kept the plans to myself, refusing to allow even Queen Victoria to see them, and I refused to build any more after Michel."

"Then how did WestTech get your plans?"

"I don't know. A few years ago, someone stole them and started an operation in Paris. I stopped them and destroyed their copies of the plans. If I had to guess, some fragments may have remained in their hands, or maybe someone remembered enough to build more, and they restarted their operations here, far from the prying eyes of England."

"And now you want to stop them?"

"Of course I do. Could you imagine what would happen if they used these machines for warfare?"

Chepi's eyes darkened. "I don't have to imagine," she said curtly. "WestTech most likely do have their sights on warfare, as they have been more than happy to test their machines on my people."

"I'm sorry. We'll stop them."

"I don't need your pity or assurances. I just need to know that you have reason to be committed to this."

Ruth raised an eyebrow. "Beyond them using my plans to murder people?"

"Forgive me if I don't want to put faith in a white woman being moved to action by my people being killed."

Ruth nodded, having to admit that Chepi had a point. "I came here with the express purpose of shutting down WestTech before I knew exactly what they were doing with my plans. That hasn't changed."

"That's good enough for me."

Ruth turned back to the facility, seeing someone in the dark.

"Who's that?" she asked.

Chepi was already moving through the greenery they were hiding in to get a better look at the figure.

"I recognise him," she said as she returned. "He's one of the regular patrons at the saloon."

"Then we can head back into town and confront him. Ask him how to get into the factory."

Chepi nodded. "That is probably a better plan than remaining here and risking being caught. We should find the others."

9

"So," Ivy said as they made their way back to the saloon, "what are we going to say to this man when we find him? We can't just start shouting at him in front of the other patrons."

Ruth shrugged. "I was just going to point my disrupter at him under the table and hope that he didn't realise that it's harmless to humans."

Sally smirked at that. "I think I'm finally warming to you."

Ruth smiled politely as they entered the establishment.

Ivy frowned, her eyes locking onto a man at the bar. "Wait... Is that James?"

Ruth looked over and saw that the man, indeed, had the same reddish-brown hair that James had, though she couldn't tell if it was him. She had never been good with faces.

"It is!" Ivy exclaimed. "That's James."

"That is also the man I saw leaving WestTech," Chepi commented as she moved to get a better look.

Ruth sighed. "If it truly is James, then I will talk to him. He may not like me, but I cannot believe he would betray the Queen like this."

Ivy raised an eyebrow. "This is the same man who tried to blackmail you, and he's working with WestTech. I think his betrayal is pretty clear."

"Fine, then I am at least certain that he would not cause a fuss in public."

"We'll be over in the corner, keeping an eye out," Sally told her before Ivy had another chance to object.

Ruth nodded, straightening her back and carefully placing her hands in front of her. She desperately wished for her dress back. Proper attire was an armour of its own. Without it, she was left with nothing but courtesy, which was something she was learned in, if not skilled.

"May I have a drink, please?" Ruth asked the bartender.

"What will you have?"

Ruth looked over the bottles, quickly coming to the conclusion that they probably wouldn't cater to her tastes, which ran decidedly non-alcoholic.

"Something strong that won't kill me," she eventually replied, deciding that asking for something weak might suggest weakness in herself that she didn't particularly want to broadcast. No, this was decidedly a rough and tumble crowd, which meant that she would have to get rough and tumble herself if she didn't want to draw unwanted attention.

The bartender nodded before pouring her a small glass of an amber liquid. She took a sip, quickly deciding that she liked the taste, even if it took everything she had to disguise her pain as it burnt on the way down.

"So, what are you doing all the way out here, James?" she asked after taking a step closer to him.

He did a double-take as he looked her over. She supposed that she might be difficult to recognise, so far from her home and comfort.

"Ruth? What the hell are you doing out here?"

"Is that really the kind of language you should use in front of a lady?" she asked in an admonishing tone, though it came out a little sharper than intended. In truth, she remained angry at James, regardless of the years that had passed. He had tried to ruin her, and he had almost succeeded.

She realised that he wasn't going to continue before she answered the question.

"Apparently someone has been copying my designs. Imagine my surprise when I saw you leaving their factory."

"I... The Queen sent you, didn't she? She sent you to stop me, but it's too late." He seemed a little manic at that.

Ruth took a slightly deeper breath than normal, using the time to decide that she was going to play along. "Too late?"

"I already sold your plans," he told her. "WestTech has them now. You've seen what they've done with those poor copies. Imagine what they could do with everything the Queen had locked away."

"I never would have taken you for a traitor, James."

He gave her an odd look before barking in laughter. "She didn't tell you, did she? She sent you after me to retrieve your plans and didn't tell you why I took them. She has played you the fool."

Ruth raised an eyebrow. "Forgive me if I won't believe that without knowing what you're talking about."

"She was going to use them."

"Use them?"

He nodded frantically. "Without being able to use your inventions for warfare, you were starting to outlive your usefulness. Better that you disappeared and she could use them without problem was her reasoning."

"So, what? You stole the plans to stop her? James, you were the one who originally wanted me to give them to her."

He frowned. "Ruth, I wanted you to sell them to her. I didn't want you to be killed over that. And... I felt that I owed you and Thomas for what I put you through."

Ruth shifted from one foot to the other. She still wasn't sure that she believed James. "So, you sold the plans to WestTech? They're hardly better than Queen Victoria."

"At least then everyone can buy your inventions, instead of just the Queen having them. It makes an even playing field."

"Anyone with *money* can buy them. That's hardly better."

"But it is still better."

Ruth sighed, having to give him that. "They're using the automatons to kill people."

"What did you think Queen Victoria was going to use them for?"

He pushed himself away from the bar, turning his back to her.

"We're not done yet," Ruth said, her hand coming to rest on her disrupter.

He turned and smirked. "Ruth, shoot me if you want, but I think we both know that you don't have the stomach for it. I'm going to get out of town so that neither WestTech nor Queen Victoria can find me. If I was you, I would do the same."

He left and Ruth made no attempt to remove her disruptor from her holster. It wouldn't do anything even if she did, and there was going to be no convincing him.

She moved to the dark corner where the other three women had set down, determination in her stride.

"I'm going to need somewhere to build," she announced.

Sally smiled. "I think I know just the place."

10

"This is my brother's place," Sally explained the next morning. They had agreed to leave their activities for the night, since a tired inventor made sloppy mistakes and that was the last thing Ruth needed.

Not that she and Ivy had managed to get much sleep after having to explain the situation to the others. They had spent their night waving off concerns about how they had managed to get themselves into such a dangerous situation and how they were out of their minds to try and do it again. In all honesty, it made Ruth question why she had started to miss people so much. They truly were the most irritating thing she ever had to deal with. And that was coming from a woman whose job frequently involved the risk of extreme burns or extremity dismemberment.

"Will your brother not mind us being here?" Ivy asked as Ruth concentrated on getting to work.

Sally smirked. "He can't protest what he doesn't know."

Ivy smiled back as she joined Ruth. Ruth had no idea what Ivy was going to put her mind to, but she trusted the other woman to make something useful and saw no need to interfere.

"Do you need us to do anything?" Chepi asked.

"No," Ivy assured them. "It's better if we're just left to work."

"A cup of tea would be nice," Ruth said.

"We're not your servants," Sally pointed out.

"You asked."

She sighed. "We don't have tea."

"Shame."

"Come on," Sally said to Chepi. "Let's leave these two to their work."

"Shouldn't we stay in case your brother returns? He won't be charitable if he finds them here."

Sally sighed and Ruth saw her glaring at them through the corner of her eye in a way that very much suggested that she would be more than happy to have her brother walk in on them alone and conclude that they had broken into his workshop.

After a few moments, however, she relented. "Fine, we'll stay. But no fetching tea," she added, loudly enough for Ruth to be sure that the comment was aimed at her.

"I only asked," she muttered to Ivy, who gave her a look that Ruth had learned meant that she had misjudged the situation, but Ivy didn't have time to explain to her how or why.

Ruth made a mental note about not asking for tea when a strange girl let you covertly use her brother's workshop.

It was several hours before they were interrupted, and Ruth was severely beginning to feel the lack of tea. Hers was hot and tiring work, which left her irritated and dehydrated.

There came a few hard thuds at the door.

"Is someone in there?"

Sally rolled her eyes. "Just me," she shouted back.

"What are you doing in my workshop, Sally?"

"Nothing you need to worry about."

Whoever was on the other side of the door - Sally's brother, Ruth presumed - didn't seem to take kindly to that, kicking the door so that it swung open, despite the flimsy latch.

A man, who looked similar enough to Sally to confirm Ruth's suspicion that they were siblings, glared at that room.

"So, what? You're starting a harem now?" he asked his sister, his voice soaked with vitriol.

She glared at him. "Don't be rude. I'm simply allowing some friends to use your workshop. They're far from home and need the workspace."

Her brother folded his arms before turning to Ruth. "Who are you?"

"I'm Ruth, and this is Ivy. We're Sally's friends."

"Sally doesn't have no friends, and I ain't never seen you before."

Ruth cringed at the use of double negatives. "We're not from around here."

"Yeah, your accent tells me that much, but not how you know my sister."

Sally sighed. "They needed a workshop, I told them you had one. They paid to use it."

"And were you ever going to tell me that, or just pocket the money yourself?"

"I was going to tell you, of course. We only made the arrangement last night."

He nodded. "Alright." He nodded to Ruth. "You seem like a respectable enough lady, and I assume you can keep your servant in line."

Ivy looked ready to curse him for his assumption, but her appreciation for the precariousness of their situation kept her quiet, though her hands were clenched into fists.

Sally's brother turned back to his sister and her lover. "Chepi's got to go. She ain't welcome here."

"She's welcome if I say she is."

Her brother gave an exasperated sigh. "Be reasonable, Sally. Do you know what they're saying about you in town? Bad enough if you were involved with a white woman, but an Indian? Do you know what they're calling you?"

"I don't care."

"Well I do, which means she has to go."

Sally stepped forward into her brother's personal space. "She stays. Unless, of course, you're willing to fight me over it."

Her brother seemed to seriously consider the option before backing down, which was the smartest thing Ruth had seen him do yet.

"One day you're going to realise I was right," he said before storming out of the workshop.

"Ignore that brute," Sally said to her lover, her voice low and soft in a way that told Ruth that she should return to her work.

"I always do."

Sally moved back over to where Ruth and Ivy were working. "So, ladies, what have you been building?"

"Tracking devices," Ivy answered. "We should be able to see automatons from a mile away."

Ruth simply indicated to one of her mechanical spiders, activating it before letting it scuttle across the workbench.

"I just need to get close enough to let my spiders loose. They should do the rest," Ruth explained.

"The rest?"

"Dismantling and exploding, where they see the opportunity."

Sally nodded, and, while she couldn't be sure, Ruth thought that she even looked impressed.

"I think I know how to get close enough," Chepi told them.

11

The plan was fairly simple. Chepi had noted that the factory had a ventilation grate on the far side from the entrance. It wasn't large enough for a person to get through, but Ruth's spiders could manage. Ruth was to go alone to avoid unwanted attention, with the others a reasonable distance behind to watch for guards. She would unleash the spiders, and they would all leave long before anyone noticed that anything was wrong.

Which was how she ended up struggling to pry open the ventilation grate in the pitch black, cursing in the most unladylike manner under her breath.

Composure was for Britain, she decided, not this far-flung, spirit-crushing land.

She sighed as she gave up on her own physical efforts, instead taking off the bag that was hanging from her shoulder. She opened it to reveal her spiders, all dormant and packed neatly on top of each other.

"Wake up," she hissed at them, causing them to scurry to life and flee the bag.

"Open the grate."

They did as they were told, carefully prying it away from the wall. Ruth gave a sigh of relief at their progress, just before she heard a click behind the grate.

"What was that?"

Before she had time to figure out, a flash of blue light erupted from the grate, blinding her.

She blinked the bright white out of her eyes, eventually regaining her sight only to see her spiders laying, inert, on the ground.

An aether bomb.

She blinked away the last spots of light from her eyes as she tried to figure out what to do. She had never quite figured out how to restore a disrupted aether core. Experiments on some of the automatons recovered from Paris showed that they could not be brought back if their core was disrupted. However, the spiders were much simpler than the automatons, and may respond to their cores being replaced.

She began to pick up the spiders, preparing to take them back, when she heard the clanging of metal footsteps approaching.

Automatons.

She reached for her disrupter, only to see that the bomb had disabled it too, its core black instead of the signature blue.

She spun around to see two automatons approaching and made a quick assessment of her situation.

Her disrupter might not fire, but it still had a long point of metal, which usually focused the aether along it. It wouldn't have been sharp enough to cause damage to a person without more force than Ruth figured she could give - though she couldn't be sure, as her knowledge of anatomy was hardly comprehensive - but there was a chance that she could use it to disrupt the flow of aether.

She thought back to her original design, quickly cycling through every available target for her blow.

After several quick iterations through the vulnerable spots, she had run out of time.

She plunged the point of the disruptor into the side of the neck of the first automaton to reach her. It spluttered and stopped, informing her that she had successfully shut it down.

She didn't have time to celebrate, however, as the second automaton didn't hesitate at its fallen comrade.

She ran back to where the others were, knowing that Ivy had a disrupter of her own, but the strength of the automaton's legs far exceeded her own, allowing it to swiftly bound up and trapped her in its metal grip.

"Let me go!" Ruth screamed as the automaton dragged her back to the factory, hoping that one of the others was at least within hearing range.

She wished that she hadn't brushed aside having one of them keep her within their sight at all times. She had thought keeping an eye further afield would give them a better head-start if guards had approached the far side of the factory.

She hadn't imagined the factory being booby trapped and automatons lying in wait for her.

Why would that have been the case, unless they had known of her plan?

The automaton stopped as Ruth saw two figures approaching. She hoped beyond hope that they were her friends, but she was disappointed to realise that they were men as they got closer.

"That's her!" one of them announced, and Ruth recognised the voice as belonging to Sally's brother.

"Yes, it is indeed," the other figure said and Ruth's blood chilled as she recognised the owner.

"*Banks*," she spat. "I should have known it was you."

"Yes, you should. For being so intelligent, you truly are dim-witted at times."

She didn't have an intelligible response, so simply gave a yelp as she tried to yank herself free from the automaton once more.

Banks responded by bringing up a small device, which sprayed her face with a fine powder.

She coughed it away, but the world swiftly melted to black.

12

Ruth awoke to find her extremities numb and her eyesight gone. After a few moments of frantic blinking, she realised that her eyesight was fine, but the room was pitch black.

She wiggled her fingers and feet in an attempt to regain feeling in them, but she found that they didn't move more than an inch or so. After a few moments, feeling returned and she realised that she was strapped down to the hard surface she was lying on.

A door opened at the far side of the room, introducing a fleck of light. Someone entered, lighting lamps as they went, illuminating the room.

"This feels awfully familiar," Ruth said, in an attempt to bolster her confidence.

The figure approached, allowing her to see that it was Banks.

"You're going to tire of kidnapping me eventually."

He smiled. "My dear, I'm already tired of it. Which is why I'll never have to do it again."

He moved his hand past her head, before she felt something large and metallic press against her skull in several places.

"What is this device you've strapped me to?" she asked, doing her best to keep alarm from her voice.

"Well, you have proven to be uncooperative, to the point at which this would be most easily solved with a well-placed bullet, but it would be such a shame to waste a brain like yours. Of course, I'm sure you know that many people have wondered about the possibility of utilising the automatons as a way to extend human life. If they have their own consciousness, why couldn't we implant them with our own?"

"Because they wouldn't be us!"

"Now, come, my dear, don't tell me that you're fretting over the soul. Surely a woman with a mind such as yours appreciates that it is a ridiculous concept made up as part of a system to keep the masses placated."

"I'm saying that it would just be a copy."

"But what is a copy, if the making of said copy kills the host? Surely, at that point, it is a transference."

Ruth struggled to keep air flowing to her lungs as she realised that he had every intention of killing her. "And what if it doesn't work? My mind will be wasted as surely as if you had used a bullet."

"No, my dear, not quite. At least, if you die like this, I can use this attempt to see that my next one is more successful."

"No, please, you're going to kill me!"

"One way or the other, that is the point," Mr Banks said as he pulled a lever by her side.

Ruth was immediately racked with the worst pain she had ever felt. Her screams echoed in her head, leaving her with just enough coherence to wonder if either death or childbirth - the two events she had always assumed were the most painful in life - could be so excruciating.

Surely not.

Mr Banks just smiled at her. "Now, my dear, you may want to save the screams. It's only warming up."

He turned back towards the door at that, leaving Ruth alone with nothing but her screams.

13

"What was that?" Ivy asked Sally as she heard a faint, high-pitched echo through the trees. "A wild animal?" she asked, hopefully.

Sally shook her head, quickly sprinting towards the sound. Ivy ran behind her, doing her best not to trip over the rough, unfamiliar terrain. Somewhere along the way, Chepi re-joined them, and Ivy felt her concern for Ruth threaten to cloud her thoughts as she did her best to refocus on not tripping up.

Sally stopped dead in her tracks, halting the other two behind her by outstretching her arms.

"What is it?" Ivy asked.

"Look," Sally prompted.

Ivy pulled her goggles down over her eyes to get a better look, despite the dark and distance.

She could see that the ventilation grate was slightly pulled away from the wall, and the spiders were lying, inert, on the ground. She flicked down a different lens, only to see pitch black. No signs of aether anywhere.

"Their aether cores were deactivated," Ivy said. "Someone must have anticipated this tactic."

"Any sign of Ruth?"

"No, nothing."

"They've probably taken her."

"So, let's go and get her back!"

Sally held her in place, stopping her from heading towards the factory.

"You'll be walking into a trap."

Chepi nodded in agreement. "If they knew that Ruth would use this entrance, they probably know that we would be with her. It would be better to return with reinforcements."

Ivy glared at both of them before turning her burning stare to the factory, as if she could clear herself a path with nothing more than her fury.

She took a deep breath before turning to the other two and nodding. "Alright. Reinforcements."

She turned away, but every step further from the factory felt like she was leaving Ruth to die.

"Do you think they're alright?" Michel asked the two men with him as they sat at the table of their room. Thomas and Hall were drinking some kind of local spirit, while Michel added his observations of them to his information on the effects of alcohol on humans.

Hall sighed, shaking his head. "As we've told you the last dozen times you have asked, we don't have any way to know."

"I know, I just..." He wrung his hands together. "I'm worried."

"So are we, but wearing your hand motors out won't help anyone."

Michel nodded in agreement as he stopped the restless motion, just in time for the door to open and reveal Ivy, with Sally and Chepi close behind.

"Michel!" Ivy exclaimed as she entered the room, running over to him and wrapping her arms around his neck as she buried her face into his chest. He quickly checked for signs of distress, such as sobbing, but he only found that she was gripping him with so much pressure that she may have hurt him if he had been human.

"They took Ruth," she told him. "They captured her."

"It's going to be alright," he assured her. "We'll get her back."

She pulled away, allowing him to see the fire in her eyes. "I know. And we're going to make them pay for taking her."

Hall stood up at that. "Perhaps it's time to consider some more upfront tactics."

Ivy nodded as she turned to him. "Get me enough aether and I can blow that place right to hell."

14

"That's it," Ivy declared several hours later, as she leaned back from the workbench. "Ten aether bombs. That's more than enough to shut down everything in the factory, with a couple for redundancy."

Michel nodded. "I'll alert the others."

"Wait," she said, stopping him in his tracks. "Michel, if we're going to be detonating aether bombs, you should stay here. You can't risk being near them."

"No, I refuse to stay here."

"Look, I know you want to get Ruth back, but we can handle it."

"And what about you? If you're worried about getting Ruth, who's going to worry about you?"

"Michel, the others will be there as well. I won't be alone."

"But I don't trust them to protect you. Thomas will put retrieving Ruth above you, Hall will put Thomas above all else, and Sally and Chepi will put stopping WestTech above all of you."

She shook her head with a smile. "And what makes you think I need protecting, Michel? I can handle myself."

"As can I, and yet you're still trying to get me to stay here. I'm expendable, Ivy. If my functioning ceases, Ruth can build another mechanical man just like me. The same cannot be said of you."

"Don't say that, Michel, you're not expendable," she told him firmly, stepping closer to him in an attempt to drive home her point.

"On the contrary, I am the very definition of expendable," he countered, closing the rest of the gap between them.

"Not to me!"

Before he had time to argue that point, her lips were on his. He had no idea what to do, and was frightened of hurting her, since his mouth wasn't designed for sensory input, so he stayed perfectly still until she pulled away.

"I'm sorry," she said, shaking her head. "I know that you don't... I just..."

He stepped back towards her, closing the gap once more before taking her hands in his, prompting her to look up at him.

"Ivy, just because I may have had to have the concept explained to me rather recently doesn't mean that I am incapable of falling in love."

She stared at him, wide-eyed and disbelieving. "So, you..."

"Ivy, I have been in love with you literally since before I knew what that meant."

"Why didn't you tell me?"

"Because you deserve a real man, not some poor facsimile."

"Michel, 'real' is something for the philosophers to debate, all I know is what's in my heart, and I love you as surely as I could love any flesh and blood man."

He smiled before pulling away a little. "I suppose that is something we can discuss once you're back."

"So you'll stay?"

"I am not happy about it, but I suppose you are right. There is too high of a chance of me being caught in the blast."

She smiled before giving him a quick peck on the cheek. "I promise that I'll return to you."

He nodded before moving his left hand to his right wrist. One of the gears had been acting up, and he had been meaning to replace it. He tugged it free from his arm, knowing that it would only slightly hinder his range of wrist motion.

"Here," he said, pressing the small gear into her palm. "So that part of me will always be with you."

"For a man who argues he's not real, you certainly have a fine grasp of sentiment," she commented as she pocketed the gear. "Thank you, Michel."

"Can you see anything?" Sally asked Ivy as they approached the factory once more.

Ivy frowned, changing her lens for a stronger one, and still seeing nothing. "There's aether and machines giving off heat, but I can't see anything resembling a person."

"It can't be abandoned."

Ivy simply shrugged.

"We stick to the plan," Hall told them. "Move out."

The others nodded, all taking their aether bombs and moving to designated points around the building. The blast of the bombs would move through the walls, shouting down any automatons or other aether-powered machines within their range.

Ivy used her pocket watch to time carefully, only detonating her bomb as the designated time arrived.

The bomb gave off a blast of blue light and she waited for the others to return.

They made their way back to her in short order, just as she had finished with the lock on the door.

"Still nothing?" Hall asked her.

"A couple of machines in the middle of the room are still active, but I can't see any sign of people."

He nodded, though seemed uneasy as he moved to kick down the door.

He moved in first, with the others coming behind him. They fanned out, checking over the powered down machinery for any sign of life.

"Maybe the factory is mostly autonomous," Sally figured.

Ivy gave a hum of agreement. "It would explain how so few people know about it."

"The question is, where is Ruth?" Thomas said.

Ivy moved around the room, looking all around with her goggles. She stopped dead as she saw a flash of blue, seemingly beneath her.

She moved back to get a better look, realising that she was seeing aether underground. When she moved too far, she lost the signal entirely, telling her that the floor was making it weak.

"Beneath us," she said. "There's something below."

Hall scouted for an entrance to the basement, finding one rather quickly.

"You girls investigate," he told them. "Thomas and I will double check for any sign of whoever did this."

Ivy nodded, heading quickly down the stairs, her disrupter drawn. The weapon cast an eerie blue glow around the room, illuminating a large contraption with a figure strapped into it. Her hair and clothes were caked to her body with sweat, and she was moaning unintelligibly.

"Ruth," Ivy said, rushing forth. She quickly found the lever to shut off the machine as Sally lit a lamp to better illuminate the room.

Ruth gave a relieved gasp, but otherwise didn't respond as the machine shut down and Ivy worked to unstrap her.

"It's okay, Ruth, I've got you," Ivy assured.

"Ivy…" her mentor managed to mumble as the final restraint was released and she almost collapsed to the floor. Ivy was the only thing propping her up.

"Come on, let's get you out of here."

Footsteps came down the stairs, and Ivy instinctively aimed her disrupter at the intruder, before realising that it was Hall.

"Whoever did this is long gone," he told them.

"Banks," Ruth managed to mumble.

"Banks?" Ivy repeated. "He locked you into that machine?"

She gave a weak nod.

"What was he trying to do?"

"Steal my brain."

Ivy didn't want to think about what she had meant by that, so she turned back to Hall.

"We need to get her out of here."

He nodded before moving to help Ivy carry her.

"We shouldn't head back to town," Sally said. "If Banks isn't here, chances are he's there. We'd be delivering her straight back."

"What do you suggest?"

"We can camp in the woods tonight. Let Ruth rest in peace. If she takes a turn for the worse, we can always go back."

Ivy and Hall nodded in agreement.

15

Everyone was already settling in for the night before Ruth felt coherent enough to form full sentences, though she still felt as if she had had one too many glasses of wine before being trampled by a horse.

She pushed herself upright against the tree Ivy had lain her next to so that she could get a better look at her friend, who appeared to be fidgeting with something metallic.

"Thank you," she managed, her voice rasping, though it was enough to draw her friend's attention.

"Pardon?"

"Thank you, Ivy. For coming to get me."

"Oh. Well, of course I did. You're my friend."

Ruth smiled, though it was barely a twitch. "Still... I appreciate it. Thank you."

"You're welcome."

Ruth glanced around the camp to see that Ivy wasn't alone. In fact, everyone had come with her, it seemed. Almost everyone.

"Where's Michel?" she asked with a frown.

"He's still in town," Ivy explained as she started fidgeting with the piece of metal again, allowing Ruth to see that it was a gear. "We used aether bombs to shut down the machines in the factory. We thought having him close was too much of a risk."

Ruth smiled as she recognised the gear in Ivy's hand as Michel's. "'We' thought, or you thought?"

Ivy gave a reluctant shrug. "I thought," she admitted. "Michel wasn't happy about it, but there was just too much risk of him being caught in one of the blasts."

"I'm glad you managed to convince him to stay. I would have hated it if any of you had been seriously hurt while retrieving me."

"We all knew the risks when we came for you. If we had been hurt, I don't think any of us would have regretted it."

Ruth decided that she was too tired to continued arguing, so she just silently nodded as Ivy returned her attention to the gear in her hands.

"He finally told you, didn't he?" Ruth asked.

"Hmm?" Ivy replied, before realising what Ruth was asking with a smile. "Of course he would have told you. How long have you known that he loved me?"

"Since just before we left England."

"I suppose that's not that long."

"So, what did you tell him?"

Ivy smiled. "That I returned his affections."

Ruth returned her smile as she settled back down. "I'm glad for the two of you."

"You should get some rest," Ivy told her.

Ruth nodded, barely managing to keep her eyes open.

Ruth awoke with a start, as she heard something rustling in the woods nearby.

She looked around the camp to see that everyone else was asleep, and she was reluctant to wake any of them up.

Especially when her mind was still fuzzy. She may have even imagined the noise.

However, just as she rolled over to try and get back to sleep, she heard the noise again.

It was probably an animal, she knew, but her confused mind refused to rest until she confirmed it.

She pushed herself up to her feet, using the tree next to her for leverage and doing her best not to disturb the others. It took her a moment to realise that she was upright, her head was still spinning, but once she was sure, she shuffled towards the noise, doing everything she could to stay on her feet.

Once she was out of view of the others, she finally happened across the source of the noise. Her eyes took a moment to adjust and recognise that it wasn't an animal in front of her. No, it was a man.

"It appears that I was right before," the man said as he raised his arm. After a moment, Ruth's eyes registered that he was pointing a gun at her. "This would have been more easily solved with a bullet."

"No," was all Ruth managed to croak out as her legs began to give beneath her. "You can't."

"You have ruined my plans for the last time," he told her.

The gun was aimed at her head, but he was moving it from side to side. It took Ruth a moment to realise that he was trying to keep up with her swaying on the spot. After a moment, he simply moved the gun down to her chest before pulling the trigger.

Ruth fell backwards into the dirt, but otherwise couldn't register what had happened.

She had been shot. That much was for certain, but anything else was thankfully blurred by her addled mind.

Maybe this is for the best, she thought as she felt what little strength she had leave her. *None of this would have happened if not for my inventions.*

"Ruth!" she heard Ivy cry as black started to bleed into her vision.

"It's okay," Ruth managed, unsure as to whether anyone was actually close enough to hear, but knowing that she had to say it anyway. "It's okay."

16

Ruth opened her eyes to find herself propped upright, surrounded by the others, with Ivy and Michel at the forefront.

"What happened?" she asked, her voice surprisingly clear, though it didn't sound like hers.

"What do you remember?" Ivy asked her.

"You rescued me from Banks, and then we were in the woods. He found us while we were sleeping. I heard him and woke up. I followed the noise, only for him to… He shot me."

Ivy nodded. "Ruth, please remain calm. We couldn't do anything for the bullet wound."

Ruth tried to frown but her face wouldn't quite respond. It felt odd. As if parts of it were numb.

Ivy simply stepped back, indicating across the room. The room Ruth now recognised as the one she had been trapped in by Banks.

She looked over to where Ivy was indicating, only to see herself, propped up in the same machine Banks had used on her. Only, the body in the machine, while it looked very much like her, was chalk white, and her bodice was stained bright red.

She wasn't breathing.

She was dead.

Ruth looked down at herself, noticing first of all that she lacked breasts. The second thing she realised was that her skin wasn't skin at all, but ceramic plates over a metal skeleton.

A standard WestTech automaton model.

"We couldn't save you," Ivy told her. "So, we used Banks' machine to save your mind. It was the best we could do. I'm sorry."

"I..." Ruth was unsure of what else to say as she stared at her hands as she moved them. Her body felt strange. Her pressure sensors were rudimentary, leaving her with far less sensation to process. She couldn't decide if that was a relief, or just unnerving.

"I can remake the body," Ivy assured her. "As soon as we've found Banks, I can make it more womanly, and I can give you every enhancement Michel has."

Ruth nodded. "Thank you," she said, in the hope that that would assure Ivy that she had done the right thing in saving her. The new body may be unnatural to her, but it was surely better than death.

Ruth attempted to step forward carefully. Everything for her height to her weight to her proportions had changed, all of which would take some getting used to.

However, her first step was a success. She quickly followed it with a second and third, gaining confidence in her new body as she went.

The new body was stronger, with larger strides.

The perfect vessel to catch Banks by his neck and return the favour, she thought as she once more dared to glance at her previous, inert form.

"Now the question is, where is Banks?" Ruth asked them.

"I think I may know how to answer that," Sally said with a fiery glare.

17

Sally took the lead as they headed back to her house, which only ruffled Ruth's feathers a little. She wanted to be the one to take revenge for what had been done to her, a fire burned just beneath her ceramic plates demanding vengeance, but there would be time for that later. Banks would be her revenge. For now, she was happy to let Sally deal with her brother.

Sally quickly spotted her brother, fast approaching him with the others in tow. They swiftly cornered him at the side of his workshop.

"Sally, what is this?" he asked, though he seemed to be sweating.

Ruth took that to mean that he knew exactly what was happening.

"You sold us out!" Sally accused. "You knew that we were going to stop WestTech and you went straight to Banks. How much did he pay you to sell out your own sister?"

"Jesus, Sally, you think I did this for money? These are dangerous people. I thought that, once you saw that, you would think twice about messing with them."

Sally responded by pushing him up against the wall of the workshop by the scruff of his neck. "I knew what I was getting into. Unlike you, I couldn't stand by and watch them roll over whoever gets in their way."

"Only because you're involved with an Indian girl! You want to pretend that you're so high and mighty, but you wouldn't even blink at WestTech if she wasn't your girl."

"Of course I would."

"Well now you're just deluding yourself. You're no better than the rest of us, you just have interests on the other side."

Sally shook her head. "Where my interests are is irrelevant. This is the right thing to do and I am doing it. Banks has hurt enough people, we're not letting him get away to start again elsewhere. Tell us where he is."

"So that he can kill you? Not a chance."

Sally responded by thrusting him up against the wall once more.

"Alright, alright!" he relented. "Banks came by and told me that he was heading out of town. He headed towards the train station."

Sally nodded, throwing him towards the ground, though he staggered a little and managed to remain on his feet.

"I have horses we can take," she told the others. "Hopefully we can catch him before the train leaves."

Ruth reached the train station first, jumping from her rather disgruntled horse as soon as it was in sight. She had never been a good rider, and she assumed that her new body only made it more uncomfortable for the horse.

As soon as her feet hit the ground, she started sprinting, her more powerful legs making for much more powerful strides.

The train station wasn't particularly large, allowing her to quickly spot Banks.

She ran up to him, and he turned to give her a confused frown as he heard her heavy metal footsteps. The second before he realised he was in peril, she grabbed him by the neck, lifting him a foot from the ground.

"Desist," he croaked. "Command override: desist!"

She grinned at that. "Oh, you don't remember me, do you?"

He stared at her with wide eyes, telling her that he had no idea what was going on.

"Let me remind you. You shot me and left me for dead."

"Ruth," he finally managed before letting out a strained laugh.

"I really don't see what's funny about your inevitable demise."

"It's funny because you won't kill me," he croaked. "You can't. Even made of metal, you're no killer."

Ruth squeezed her fingers a little around his neck, but not enough to truly do harm. She wanted to draw this out, she told herself. Of course she would kill him. She couldn't not.

She moved to crush his neck, but her hand refused to obey as she felt in icy chill down her spine.

She had to do it. She had to make sure that he didn't just start somewhere else.

But her hand refused to move.

No, she refused to move it.

Even faced with Banks' smug face, she couldn't end it.

"She may not be a killer," she heard past Banks. "But I know how to put a stray dog down."

The next thing Ruth knew, there was a hole through Bank's head.

She dropped him to the ground, revealing Hall standing behind him with a gun in his hand.

"I had that handled," she eventually said as she processed what had happened.

"Of course," he said. "Are you alright?"

She looked down at herself in an attempt to assess any potential damage. She didn't seem to have any damage, but she was drenched in bright red blood, though she had no way of feeling it.

"I believe so," she told him before reaching down to Banks' body. As she rolled him over, she quickly found her plans.

"Is that all of them?" Hall asked.

She nodded. "I believe so."

"Then we have exactly what we came for."

18

Ruth watched the flames of the bonfire reach for the night sky for several moments, wondering if she could ever sacrifice enough to the flames to reach the stars.

As if to test her pondering, she threw her plans onto the bonfire, one by one.

"Wait," Thomas said, placing his hand over hers as she got to the third piece of paper. "Are you sure?"

She nodded. "I had always hoped that, at some point, there would be someone that I trusted enough to bestow these plans to. But I don't think that day will ever come. Given that I am now, essentially, immortal, and these plans are firmly secured in my mind, it is better to destroy these. If the day ever comes when I am comfortable enough to pass them on, I can always draw them up again."

Thomas nodded, stepping back and allowing her to throw the rest of them to the flames.

"So, back to England?" Ivy asked.

Ruth shook her head. "Not for me," she told them. "If James was right, I'm not safe anywhere. I doubt that my new body will change that. It would be best for everyone if I simply disappear."

"Disappear?" Michel asked. "Where will you go?"

"The factory here is abandoned now, and it's far enough out of the way that most will ignore it. I can work out of it as much as I like without interacting with anyone else, since I don't need food anymore."

"Are you sure?" Ivy asked. "You'll be cut off from everyone else."

Ruth nodded. "It's for the best." She turned to the others. "What about all of you? The chances are, you'll be under suspicion for my disappearance."

"I think it's about time to retire," Hall told her before turning to Thomas. "France is usually nice this time of year."

Thomas nodded with a smile, taking his love's hand. "I think retirement is exactly what's in order."

"Just as long as you're happy," Ruth told them before turning to Ivy and Michel. "And what about you two?"

"Well, I doubt our relationship will be accepted, even in France," Michel ventured.

Ivy nodded. "Perhaps disappearing isn't the worst idea in the world."

"Disappearing?" Ruth echoed. "Disappearing where?"

"Well, the factory is more than big enough for the three of us, isn't it?" she asked Ruth. "If that's fine with you, of course."

"Of course it is, but are you truly okay with being hidden away from everyone? From all of society? Not to mention, tolerance may be hard to find, but America is hardly the best place to start."

Ivy shrugged. "Then we'll try it for now. If it turns out to be a terrible idea, we can always head elsewhere later. But, for now, I think here is a good place to settle."

Michel nodded. "It seems as good a place as any."

"Then I guess we'll see," Ruth said as she looked back to the stars, wondering what the future may hold.

Want to read the Epilogue short story?

Visit lcmawson.com/LadyRuthEpilogue to get your free copy!

Made in the USA
Middletown, DE
08 February 2017